TOBY AND THE

WIZARDS OF WILDHAVEN

by

Sally Doherty

Cover illustration and internal illustration by Sarah Jane Docker

www.sarahjanedocker.com

Formatting by Let's Get Booked

www.letsgetbooked.com

Proofreading by Noble Owl

www.nobleowlproofreading.co.uk

Print ISBN: 978-1-9196259-2-8

eBook ISBN: 978-1-9196259-3-5

Ten percent of author profits from each book will be donated to the ME Association.

This is the second book in the Toby Bean trilogy.

Have you read the first book?

Toby and the Silver Blood Witches

Winner of the Book Bloggers' Novel of the Year Award 2022

and WriteBlend Middle Grade Book Awards 2022

Shortlisted for The Selfies Book Awards 2022 and

The Rubery Book Award 2022

Finalist for the Wishing Shelf Awards 2021

Praise for

Toby and the Wizards of Wildhaven:

"Witches, wizards, potions, and peril. Sally Doherty has done it again - Toby is back, and this time his adventure is more dangerous and exciting than ever! Impossible to put down, it needs a warning that it may cause torchlit reading escapades to race to the finish."

Lisette Auton, author of The Secret of Haven Point and The Stickleback Catchers

"An exciting broomstick ride into magic, new friendships, and betrayal."

Emma Read, author of Milton the Mighty and The Housetrap

"A thrilling whirlwind of magic, courage, and friendship that had me on the edge of my seat."

Jenny Moore, Author of Emba Oak and the Terrible Tomorrows

"Sally Doherty weaves a spellbinding story of charming magical characters, an action-packed plot, and a brave young carer."

Kate Heap, Primary English Consultant and book blogger

"Toby Bean is one of the most important and real characters around. So many children will feel the quiet joy at finally seeing themselves being represented, while other readers will gain invaluable insight into another life."

Mr Tarrant, Year 5/6 teacher, Assistant Head and English lead

For my dad,

love you always

CHAPTER ONE

Toby's tummy was as empty as a leaky cauldron. He gazed at the shop shelves with their rows of chocolate bars, gleaming in their shiny wrappers. He could almost taste the milky cocoa, feel it melt on his tongue and ooze down his throat. Lunch had been a dry sandwich and not much else. He and Mum hardly had any money for food, and as for the witches, their cooking was as tasty as a pile of potato peelings.

A boy barged past and grabbed one of the bars. How much did they cost? Seventy pence. Toby counted the change in his pocket. Twenty pence. *Twenty measly pence*. That was all he had. Why had he even come in here?

His stomach rumbled loudly, and he glanced up, but the shopkeeper was busy serving the boy. Without thinking, Toby seized a bar and slipped it down his sleeve. He hurried through the crowd of school kids and out of the shop, his cheeks burning. Fighting a desperate urge to break into a run, he strolled away.

Out of sight, Toby removed the wrapper and shoved the bar into his mouth. It was his favourite: chocolate filled with caramel and bursting with nuts, yet it made him feel sick. The creamier the chocolate, the richer the caramel and the crunchier the nuts, the guiltier he became. Voices sounded round the corner, and Toby almost choked on the bar. It stuck in his throat, and he had to take great gulps to force it down.

Even after he'd swallowed, his throat still felt tight. Toby pulled at the neck of his school jumper to give himself air. He needed to chill out. He was getting in a state – his chest was feeling tight now too. The material prickled through his shirt, pressing against his skin. Toby glanced at it.

Wait a minute.

His jumper seemed to be shrinking. The V-neck opening hugged his neck, and the sleeves now finished halfway up his forearms and were cutting off his circulation. Toby squirmed, trying to break free. This was a new jumper. His old one had become so tattered it resembled Bumble's bat. They hadn't been able to afford to buy one, so Witch Hazel had knitted it. *What the heck had she done to it?*

Toby tugged at the jumper in growing alarm, but it wouldn't budge. It was getting smaller and smaller, wrapping itself around him like a boa constrictor.

He started to run. He raced along street after street, past his old house on Fir Tree Close and into the run-down estate where he and Mum now lived. Toby took a shortcut through a narrow passageway between backyards, his jumper growing tighter by the second. It was a good job he was a fast runner. He nearly didn't make it though. By the time he reached his road, he was having to stop every few metres to wheeze and pull the material away from his windpipe.

Bursting through the kitchen door, Toby collapsed on the floor where he lay writhing, the jumper squeezing the oxygen out of his body.

"Mercy me!" Witch Hazel pulled her wand from her pocket in panic. The stick slipped from her trembling fingers, the pointed end spearing Toby's leg. "S... Sorry!" Hazel scooped up the wand and chanted:

Free this boy
Stop your fight
Release your grip
And end his fright.

The jumper slackened, leaving Toby spluttering in a heap. Slowly, it grew and grew until it had regained its normal size. Pins and needles filled Toby's arms as the blood flowed back. When his breathing had returned to its usual rhythm, he pulled himself to his feet. "What is wrong with this jumper?!"

"I'm so sorry, Toby," said Hazel, stray wisps of white hair escaping from her bun and her spectacles askew on her nose. "I must have used behavioural wool. In the past, it was used to discipline unruly witchettes. Witch Willow doesn't agree with such measures these days. But I found a whole stock cupboard full of it in Little Witchery, and I thought there was no point in letting it go to waste. I see its effects are a little extreme..." She tailed off.

"A little extreme? You almost killed me!" Toby yanked off the jumper and flung it onto a kitchen chair.

"It was lucky I was here." Hazel paused. "What did

you do anyway? Behavioural wool doesn't act like that for nothing."

Toby clamped his mouth shut and stormed out of the kitchen.

"What the flapping fluttermice is going on?" asked Witch Bumble, bustling out of the lounge.

Toby pushed past her and climbed the narrow stairs to his room. Everything was such a mess. And now he'd made it worse. He'd stolen. It might only have been a bar of chocolate, but he'd still stolen. He hadn't needed to be suffocated by a jumper to know he'd done the wrong thing.

"Toby?" His mum called from the next bedroom.

He always popped in to see her after school. It couldn't be fun lying in bed, feeling poorly all day. But he couldn't face her right now. Toby stared out of his cracked window onto the row of tiny, two-bed terraced houses. He hated this street with its grey brickwork, missing roof tiles and not a plant or tree in sight. At the end of the road, traffic roared past. It was so noisy it made the glass rattle. How was Mum supposed to rest?

Toby threw himself onto his bed. This place was so different from their old, comfortable home. Not for the first time, he wondered if he'd done the right thing saving Witch Skylark from the claws of the Society of Magical Investigation last summer. If only she hadn't destroyed the SMI building. Mum wouldn't have lost her income, and they wouldn't have had to move.

Knock knock. Bumble poked her head into his bedroom.

"Go away," hissed Toby.

"We won't be a minute." She flung open his door

and trotted in, her multicoloured patchwork dress billowing around her. Barnaby, her bat, flew from her pocket and landed on Toby's shoulder. He nuzzled Toby's cheek before swinging upside down.

"See, he's trying to cheer you up," grinned Bumble. "He's the best fluttermouse ever."

Toby scowled but reached out a finger and stroked Barnaby's furry chest.

"We know this year has been tough, Toby." Witch Hazel edged into the room behind Bumble. "And most of it is our fault."

"Skylark's fault!" interrupted Bumble. "She's the one who burnt down the SMI."

"Anyway," continued Hazel. "We wanted to do something to say thank you."

Toby shifted uncomfortably. "You already help twice a week so that I can go to football. That's more than enough."

"We brought you some tibtabs." Hazel handed him a bundle of cloth. "This is the first batch of the year. I know they're your favourite."

Toby undid the bundle and pulled out a purple fruit in the shape of a teardrop. "Thanks." He peeled the pointed end apart and squirted the syrupy liquid into his mouth. It was as delicious as the one he'd tried in Little Witchery. At least the witches had one food which tasted good.

"I'm sorry there's not many." Hazel directed a glare at Bumble, who had purple smeared around her lips. "*Someone* got hungry on the flight here." Hazel might be soft-spoken and tiny, but she could be fierce when she wanted to be.

Bumble hastily wiped her face with the sleeve of her cloak. "There's something else! We want to invite you on holiday."

"Holiday?" Toby's eyes widened.

"Yes, with the wyline clan." Bumble beamed.

"A holiday with *all* the witches?" Toby recoiled. No way was he going on that. It was good of Bumble and Hazel to help out occasionally, and their company was … well, interesting to say the least … but one week with several hundred witches? No, thank you very much.

CHAPTER TWO

Bumble nodded enthusiastically, her chestnut hair bouncing in its loose bun. "Yes. We're going on our annual trip to the wizards in two weeks. During your school holidays."

"I can't leave Mum," said Toby. She was no better. If anything, she was worse after the stress and upheaval of moving house. If only his dad were alive to help.

Witch Hazel stepped forwards. "I'm going to stay with her. It's all worked out. And you need the break."

Toby frowned. It was true; he could do with some time off and a chance to get away for a bit. But this wasn't a holiday to explore a tropical island. Nor was it a trip with his mates to a football camp. This was a holiday with a troop of middle-aged witches on broomsticks, with black cloaks and peculiar ways.

"We'll be by the sea!" said Bumble.

"Whereabouts?" asked Toby.

"Can't say. It's top secret."

"Come on, tell me."

For once, Bumble was tight-lipped. She shook her head firmly. "We have to take an oath never to reveal its location. Like the one we take for Little Witchery."

"Will it be warm?" Toby looked outside at the grey sky. It had rained so much this summer.

"Um… it's not *that* cold."

"Do the wizards play football?" asked Toby.

"Which one's that again?" Bumble knitted her brow.

"You know! You kick a ball."

"Oh, well, maybe not that exactly," said Hazel, "but don't worry, they play all sorts of games."

"It'll be fun! Wait till we arrive." Bumble's face lit up. "They have a big fire burning for our welcome feast, and we all dance around the flames."

Dance around a fire? Toby had visions of them beating their chests and shaking straw skirts.

"You'll see Wizard Shield juggling flares too. He's our expert flame thrower. Makes him one of their best security measures. No one could get past him."

Toby drew back. This was *not* making him want to go.

Hazel patted his shoulder. "They won't attack *you*. They're our families. They know you helped us."

She took Bumble's arm and steered her towards the bedroom door. "We'll leave you to consider it. I'll cook some nice sprugel soup before football tonight."

"Um, thanks." Toby's stomach convulsed. *Ugh.* Apart from tibtabs, wyline food must be the most disgusting on the planet.

He sat on his bed thinking. A break *would* be good. Plus, it would give him a chance to ask Witch Willow about making money out of magic. Hazel and Bumble said it wasn't possible, but maybe Willow would have the answer. She was Head Witch, after all. Then again, maybe there'd be the chance to ask her another time. It would be more fun to spend the summer with Roger and Jazz.

Toby peered into his mum's room.

She opened her eyes and smiled at him from the pillows. "Hi, love." Her voice was husky – she would have hardly spoken all day.

"Hazel mentioned a holiday. But I'm not going to go," said Toby.

She cleared her throat. "You should!"

"I'd prefer to be with Roger and Jazz."

His mum's face fell. "Roger's mum sent me a message today. I'm afraid they're going to Mauritius."

"What!"

"They've been saving for ages, and some last-minute cheap flights have come up. Sorry, love."

"How long for?"

She bit her lip. "A month."

"A month!" Black clouds descended over Toby.

"They're staying with family. It's important they see them. They haven't been for a long time."

Toby flopped onto the side of the bed. A whole summer holidays without his friends.

"Going away with the witches doesn't sound so bad now, huh?" said his mum.

"Guess not," muttered Toby. Maybe he should go. "Are you sure you wouldn't mind?"

"I can't pretend I like the idea of you flying several hundred feet above the ground with only a stick beneath you. But it will do you good to have a change." She reached for his hand. "I'm just sorry I can't take you anywhere myself."

17

"Yeah, me too." Toby took her hand. Human touch still seemed alien after bottling up his feelings for two years since Mum fell ill. But it was warm and comforting too.

"Do you remember we used to go and stay in the caravan in Wales?" she said.

"Of course!"

"I could never get you out of the sea. You loved it in there. Even when you were turning blue."

They grinned at each other, and then sadness trickled through Toby. Memories were nice, but they were always tinged with sorrow. Who knew if he'd be able to go on holiday with Mum ever again?

"I'm sorry *you* won't get a change of scenery." Toby pulled back the frayed curtain. The view was bleak: endless small, concreted gardens. "I shouldn't have rescued Skylark. At least you could see grass from your old window." It started to rain outside, and there was a drip, drip, drip as droplets fell through the ceiling into a bucket. "This can't be good for you! It's all my fault."

His mum heaved herself to a sitting position. "We've been through this! I know this place isn't ideal. But you absolutely did the right thing." She squeezed his arm. "You saved Skylark's life! And Daisy's. I'm so proud of you." She paused. "And just think, if you hadn't, we wouldn't have Bumble and Hazel helping us. Don't you love eating nimnuckets and sprugels?" She winked at him, and they burst out laughing.

"Will you be OK with Hazel looking after you for a whole week if I go away?" said Toby.

"I'll be fine. Just make sure you show her how to work the cooker … again."

Toby rolled his eyes. Even after months, he couldn't be sure if he'd get home from football to find the kitchen splattered in blue sprugel goo.

"So it's decided? You're definitely going?" His mum regarded him expectantly.

Toby groaned. "Yes, yes, I'll go." Before he'd even finished saying the words, he knew he'd live to regret it.

CHAPTER THREE

A week later, Toby walked home from school, spinning a football. "I can't believe you're going to Mauritius for a whole *month*," he said to Roger and Jazz.

"Wish you could come," said Roger.

"I can't leave Mum. Anyway, we could never afford the flight."

"It's been so long since we saw Dada and Dadi-Ma!" Jazz jumped up and down, her black ponytail swinging.

A stab of envy shot through Toby. Roger and Jazz were his best friends in the world, and their families always welcomed him with open arms. But it wasn't the same as being part of a family himself. Roger and Jazz were cousins and had brothers and sisters, aunts and uncles, grandparents and more. All Toby had was Mum.

"Are you going to be able to get a holiday?" Roger asked.

"I might be going away for a week, actually." Toby threw the football to Jazz.

"Awesome!" she said, catching it and chucking it to Roger. "Who with?"

"Um…" Toby paused. *Why had he said anything?* His friends had no idea the witches existed, no idea at all.

"Um… With an old relative… In the North."

Roger threw the football back to Toby. "Sounds … fun?"

"Yeah." Toby shrugged. "It'll be a change, at least." He lobbed the ball to Roger.

"Ow!" It hit Roger on the head and bounced over a gate.

"Why weren't you watching?" cried Toby.

"Why weren't *you* watching?" retorted Roger.

They peered over the ornate gate. A drive led to a large house with perfectly manicured gardens. In the centre stood a fountain and two bushes pruned in the shape of peacocks.

"Who lives here?" said Jazz, eyes wide.

Roger gritted his teeth. "I think it's Dacker's."

Dacker? Their arch-enemy? Of all the places to choose. *Drat. Mega drat.* Toby gave Roger a push. "You better get the ball before anyone sees us."

"I'm not getting it! You're the one who threw it. And you're better at climbing than me."

"No way!" said Toby. Ever since he'd got the better of Darren Dackman last summer, the boy had largely left him alone. But trespassing in his garden was asking for trouble.

"We could always leave the ball," said Jazz.

Toby sighed. They couldn't do that. Good footballs were expensive, and he couldn't afford another one. "Keep watch," he said and hauled himself onto the iron gate. Using the pattern of spirals as footholds, he clambered over.

The ball had rolled several metres along the drive. Toby's feet scrunched on the gravel as he tiptoed towards it. He was picking it up when Roger hissed, "Look out!" and pointed towards the house.

A gleaming black BMW sat in front of the fountain. One of its doors swung open, and out stepped a boy with fair hair. *Dacker.*

Toby darted into the bushes on the edge of the drive. Had Dacker seen him? No, he was too engrossed in his phone. Two more figures climbed from the car. Mr Dackman – Dacker's dad – and … who was the other man? His white beard was so long the tip brushed his belt. And what was he wearing? With blue and white stripes, his top and trousers looked like pyjamas rather than daytime clothes.

There was something else odd about him too. Dacker's dad barked a few words, and the man jumped as if he was scared. He removed a bag from the boot, but his hand was trembling so much that he dropped it. A bottle rolled out with a clatter. And then it happened. As the man bent to pick up the bag, the bottle rolled back in without being touched.

Toby frowned. Did it move by itself? As he parted the leaves to get a better view, a twig broke with a loud snap.

"Hey!" shouted Dacker. "There's someone in the bushes!"

Toby's heart missed a beat. He'd have to make a run for it. Clutching the football, he darted down the drive and scrambled over the gate. "Just getting my ball," he called when safely on the other side.

Mr Dackman charged towards them, snorting like an angry rhinoceros. "This is private property. How dare you sneak around. Clear off the lot of you!"

As they scuttled away, Toby had a last glimpse of the man standing at the top of the drive, his face pale and his mouth open as if he was trying to call out to them.

They stopped round the corner, panting for breath.

"That was close!" spluttered Roger.

"Why did it have to be Dacker's house?" said Toby. "He won't let us forget it."

Jazz patted him on the shoulder. "Holidays now. No school. We won't have to see him."

"Hmm."

When his breathing had returned to normal, Toby cleared his throat. "Did you see the man they were with?"

"Kind of," said Roger. "We were a bit far away, though. Why?"

"He seemed sort of … well … strange."

"Strange?" asked Jazz.

"He was scared of something. And the bottle … it rolled back into the bag by itself."

"By itself?" Roger's eyes sparkled. "Maybe it was lying on a caterpillar, or maybe an army of ants was carrying it, or maybe–"

"He's off again!" interrupted Jazz. "It was probably on a slope."

She was right. Just because Toby knew witches existed, he was imagining magic everywhere now.

"What do you want to do for the first day of the holidays?" said Jazz. "Meet in the park tomorrow morning?"

Toby paused. It was still hard to leave Mum alone when he wasn't at school, but he was getting better at it. She would be fine without him; the quiet was good for her. "Sure."

"Bring your bike," called Roger as they separated. "We can explore the woods."

Toby trudged towards his house, but for once, he didn't notice the cramped streets. He couldn't get the odd man out of his head. Even if the bottle had been on a slope, what about his clothes, the trembling fingers? And there was something else. The final look he'd shot had burnt into Toby's retinae. The man's eyes had been large and pleading, his mouth gaping. Had he been trying to say something? Had he been crying for help?

CHAPTER FOUR

On the way to meet Roger and Jazz the next morning, Toby took a detour to his old road, Fir Tree Close. The incident at the Dackers' house plagued his thoughts. The strange man's silent shout had sparked a memory in Toby – a witch standing at the SMI window several years ago, crying for help. Mr Dackman used to work for the SMI. And now he had a frightened man doing jobs for him. Was something going on? Was the SMI up to its old tricks again? Toby had to check, make sure the Society really was gone for good.

Not much had changed on the close. The large, metal SMI gates still hung on the corner, though the sign had been removed. And there were the same semi-detached redbrick houses around a cul-de-sac.

A car drove past and pulled into the drive of number twelve – Toby's house. Only it wasn't his house anymore. A teenage boy and his dad climbed out of the car, and the man gave his son a pat on the shoulder. Jealousy seeped through Toby. He rubbed his finger over his top lip where the faintest whisker of hair was growing. When should he start shaving? How was he supposed to shave? These were the things a father was supposed to help you with. But his dad had died in a car accident when Toby was two. It seemed the older Toby became, the more he missed having a dad, and the more he needed one in his life.

He gave himself a shake – he hadn't come here to gawp at his old home and mourn the past. He turned to look at the old SMI entrance. There used to be no way past the gates, but now they hung slightly ajar. Checking no one was watching, Toby pushed them, and they opened with a familiar creak. The noise triggered a tornado of emotions. He hadn't been here since last year, but everything flooded back: Skylark and Daisy imprisoned behind bars. The organisation that would kill to find out how magic worked. The operating theatre. The jars of witch blood. And then the fire, blisteringly hot and raging through the building.

Toby's throat felt tight as if the smoke was once again choking his lungs. Horror pulsed through him, and he swallowed it down. That was all over. Skylark and Daisy were safe now.

He tiptoed a few paces into the SMI grounds: it was a wasteland. The building had been completely destroyed by the fire, and only mounds of charred rubble remained. Weeds and knee-high thistles engulfed the once immaculate lawn.

Toby walked in further, sidestepping bricks and broken glass. He kicked a pile of stones, and there was a clang as his shoe hit metal. What was that? He rummaged through the debris, and half of a large satellite dish emerged, covered in soil. *The witch detector.* Toby stood up, wiping his palms on his trousers. *Well, that settled it.*

Without the detector, the SMI wouldn't be able to capture any more witches. As for the strange man, he was probably a relative of the Dackmans. And who wouldn't look scared living with them? Toby suppressed a smile. Or maybe he was a childminder for Dacker's younger brother? That could be it. Mr Dackman must be a terrifying boss.

Toby headed out of the grounds, pulling the gate closed behind him. He never wanted to return. It wasn't a surprise he was still traumatised by last summer's events, but it was clear the SMI had gone. Feeling lighter, Toby retrieved his bike from the pavement. He could enjoy the holidays, and who knew, maybe it would even be fun with the wizards. He sprang onto his bike and pedalled off to meet his friends. Everything was going to be fine.

CHAPTER FIVE

Squashed behind Bumble on her broomstick the following Saturday, Toby clenched his teeth. It had been a year since he'd flown on a broom, and he'd forgotten how much he hated it. Unlike the previous blazingly hot summer, this July had been wet and blustery, and August seemed to be going the same way. The broom rocked, and Toby's cornflakes threatened to make a reappearance.

With Bumble's patchwork dress and cloak taking up almost the entire broom, Toby perched on the bristly end. The spikes poked him in the bottom, and his heart hovered in his mouth. If he slipped backwards just a couple of centimetres, he would fall off and plummet to the ground. He clung to Bumble's middle and willed the journey to end.

"We're nearly there!" shouted Bumble after an hour of flying, the wind whipping the words away.

Toby breathed a sigh of relief. The surrounding air darkened, and they flew through a sort of tunnel before popping out into the entrance hall to Little Witchery. Bumble performed her usual clumsy dismount, staggering forwards and colliding with the wall. Toby fell off the broomstick and collapsed in a grateful heap.

He scanned the small, high-ceilinged room. He'd only been here once, and he certainly never expected to be returning. There was no witch on sentry duty, so Bumble inserted her wand into a hole in the wall. The intricate system of cogs whirred, and slowly, the grand oval doors opened.

Either side of the door crouched Howler and Growler, the two stone gargoyles. They faced each other with evil grins and stubby wings curling from their backs. Toby knew what to expect, but still, he flinched as yellow flares fired out of their mouths, striking the opposite walls.

Bumble counted:

One, two
Shots through
Three, four
And some more

Toby got into position, ready to run after number ten, but Bumble grabbed his wrist. "Change of pattern!"

Five
Jump!
Six
Duck!

Bumble yanked Toby down, but he was too slow. A shot streaked over his head, scorching his hair, and an acrid smell filled the air.

Seven, eight
Don't be late!

She dragged Toby past the gargoyles and through the doors as they clanged shut behind them.

Toby ran his hand over his head, and a clump of singed strands fell to the floor. "You could have told me what to expect!"

"I did," said Bumble.

"I mean in advance! Not right in the middle of it."

Bumble ruffled his hair, and several more locks fell off. "Flapping fluttermice!"

"Is it bad?" asked Toby.

"Um… You have a bit of a gap."

"A gap?"

"I wouldn't worry; you can just see a patch of your scalp."

"WHAT!" Toby already had an unusual white tuft above the nape of his neck. Now he was bald too?

"I can fix it." Bumble held her wand aloft.

Fill this gap
Regrow the hair
Nice and thick
Sunny and fair.

"Sunny and fair?" cried Toby. "My hair's brown."

"Yes, I see that now." Bumble chewed her lip.

"What have you done?"

"Nothing!"

"I need a mirror."

"Well, I don't have one," said Bumble.

30

Toby rummaged in his backpack.

"What are you doing? We have to get on."

"I'm looking for my phone. I need to check my hair."

Bumble tugged Toby's arm. "No time! We're late."

He sighed, slung his bag over his shoulder, and stepped into Little Witchery, blinking in the light after the dark entrance hall. The large transparent dome stretched above them. It was cloudy here, like outside, but there was no hint of wind. The characterful town with its odd-shaped houses spread before them like a colourful, higgledy-piggledy eiderdown. Nothing much had changed since last year, but the sight still made Toby gape in wonder.

"Come on!" said Bumble. "They're waiting for us."

Toby stopped in his tracks. Assembled on the nearby green stood the entire wyline clan draped in their black cloaks. At Toby's appearance, a murmur stirred through the group like a sharp breeze on a still day.

Then two shadowy shapes swooped out of the sky and dug their talons into Toby's ears. Pain seared through him. Before he could react, he was lifted into the air. He dangled above the ground, screaming in agony. Surely, his ears couldn't hold his whole weight? They must be stretching and stretching. Maybe they'd rip off entirely. He reached up, trying to detach the claws from his flesh, but they wouldn't let go.

The Head Witch's voice rang out:

Free this boy
He means no harm
Release your grip
And end his alarm.

31

Toby plummeted to the floor, and the two cravens flapped, shrieking into the sky.

"Bumble!" said the Head Witch, Willow. "You were supposed to forewarn us of your arrival, so I could lift the new security measures."

"I'm sorry! I forgot. I was distracted trying to get past Howler and Growler." Bumble ripped a patch from her dress and leant over Toby, wiping the blood from his ears.

"I thought this was meant to be a holiday." Toby got shakily to his feet. "That's the second time today you've tried to kill me."

"Come." Willow beckoned. She was tall and slender with a mass of voluminous orange curls.

Toby approached cautiously, keeping a close watch on the yellow flowers with three heads. Last year, they'd puffed clouds of gas at him.

"Don't worry," said Willow. "It's safe now."

She turned to address the crowd. "Sisters, this is Toby. As you know, he will be joining us on our holiday. We owe him much gratitude for rescuing Skylark last summer, and I ask you to make him most welcome."

Hundreds of pairs of eyes stared suspiciously at Toby, and his face flushed as red as his ears. He had a strong desire to run back into the entrance hall. He would have done just that if he hadn't been rooted to the spot.

"Don't mind them," whispered Bumble. "They don't trust Earthens, but they'll get used to you."

Willow attempted to recapture the witches' attention with the roll-call. "Witch Waffle?"

"Here!"

"Witch Holly?"

"Here!" Toby's old next-door neighbour, Mrs Winterberry, raised an arm. It was still a surprise she'd turned out to be a witch. She gave Toby a small wave before disappearing into the throng.

A scroll of paper danced in front of Willow. Each time a witch answered, a line would cross through their name with a spark of silver.

"Witch Ebonia? … Ebonia?" Willow scanned the faces around her.

A witch with long ebony hair and cold green eyes stepped forwards.

Toby racked his brain. Where had he seen her before? A memory came to him. She'd tried to take over the position of Head Witch from Willow last year. She didn't think the witches should have to hide away in the sky – she'd wanted to lead them to war against Earthens!

"I will not be joining you," said Ebonia.

A hush fell over the crowd.

"I'm sorry?" said Willow.

"I do not feel well. And besides, I have no family

33

amongst the wizards."

Willow arched an eyebrow. "Perhaps one of our Protectors will stay with you?" She turned to a group of elderly witches, each of whom attempted to evade her gaze and melt into the background.

"Protectors care for sick witches," Bumble whispered.

"Witch Hazel is one, isn't she?" said Toby.

Bumble nodded.

Eventually, one of the Protectors spoke up. "If you don't mind, Witch Willow, we've been looking forward to this trip ever so long. We'd all really like to go and see our families."

"Of course, I'm sorry." Willow tapped her finger against her thigh.

"Don't concern yourself. I don't intend to take control of your office while you're away." Ebonia gave a short laugh.

No one joined in.

An icy atmosphere hung in the air.

Toby shivered.

Bumble bit her lip so hard she drew blood.

Willow drew herself up to her full height. "I will not allow you to remain here alone."

"I do not take orders from you. If I'm ill, I have the right to remain behind, per Wyline Council rules."

Another witch motioned Willow aside. They talked animatedly for several minutes, referring to a thick document that hovered next to them. Mouth pursed, Willow faced Ebonia. "Will Gemeralda be coming?"

"She will." Ebonia pushed forwards a witch of about thirteen who shared her raven black locks and startlingly emerald eyes. "I trust you will look after my daughter in my absence." Then Ebonia melted into the crowd.

Willow resumed the roll-call, a new sharp edge to her voice.

"Is Ebonia still trying to take control of Little Witchery?" Toby asked Bumble.

"She hasn't tried since she lost the vote last summer." Bumble paused. "Come to think of it – I've hardly seen her around much lately. I don't know where she's been. It's odd for her to miss our annual trip; she usually wants to take a leading role in everything."

"You don't think she still wants to attack Earthens … do you?"

"I doubt it. How could she do that by herself? But I don't like the idea of her staying in Little Witchery alone. I don't like it one bit." Bumble wrung her hands. "Bubbling cauldrons, I wonder what she's up to."

CHAPTER SIX

As Willow neared the end of the roll-call, the clan hustled and bustled, fastening cloaks and preparing broomsticks. Every now and then, Toby caught a witch staring at him, and his skin prickled. He may have got to know Bumble and Hazel over the last year, but the rest were strangers – strangers with powerful magic.

To one side, Ebonia was deep in discussion with her daughter. Toby strained to hear against the background of excited chatter.

"You have everything you need?" murmured Ebonia.

Gemeralda darted a glance at Willow before opening the top of a small sack to show a bundle of rope peeping out of the top.

Weird. What did she need that for?

Toby checked around. He was the only one who'd noticed.

"Are you sure we're doing the right thing?" said Gemeralda.

"Absolutely. Remember what they did to your grandmother." Ebonia placed her palm under her daughter's chin. "You know the plan. Good luck, my dear."

Plan? What plan?

Toby watched as Ebonia walked away, disappearing into the town.

Willow flicked her wand, and the scroll of paper rolled up and whizzed down her sleeve. She gazed at the retreating figure of Ebonia, then strode over to Toby and took his hand with a smile. "So glad you could join us." She indicated the top of his head. "New fashion?"

"We had a slight incident with Howler and Growler," mumbled Bumble.

"I see."

Toby ran his fingers through his hair. Was it really that bad?

He opened his mouth to reply, but Willow had already slipped into the throng of witches, muttering, "Now, where is she…"

The Head Witch materialised several seconds later, gripping the arm of a young witch. "Toby, this is Witch Flame-Red, my daughter."

The explanation was unnecessary – with Flame-Red's orange curls, it was clear they were related. But while Willow's hair, despite its volume, remained smart and under control, her daughter's was a wild and untamed mane. Unlike the other witches, who all seemed to wear dresses, Flame-

Red was wearing a knitted red jumper and blue trousers.

"Flame-Red is the same age as you," said Willow. "You will be travelling on her broom." She gave her daughter a nudge. "Go on then. Attach his bag."

Flame-Red scowled. Obviously, she had the temperament of a lion to match her mane. "Why am I the one who has to fly with an Earthen?"

"Flame!" exclaimed Willow in a do-not-dare-disobey-me voice, her grey eyes glinting.

Without looking at Toby, Flame-Red took his bag and fastened it to her broom.

Bumble was studying the disc which hung at her neck. "Still no warbler message from Wizard Merrycheeks. He hasn't replied for weeks. He'd better have a good excuse!"

"My dad and brother haven't been replying to Mum's messages either," said Flame-Red.

Bumble gave her warbler a shake. "Maybe they're broken."

"They're probably all too busy preparing for our visit," said her sister, Witch Wing, joining them.

It was weird the witches and wizards didn't live together. But whenever Toby asked why, Bumble said it was a long story. Bearing in mind she could talk for England, it must be a long story indeed – either that or she was hiding something.

"Take your positions!" shouted Willow, and all around them, witches rose into the air, forming a line two by two.

Flame-Red mounted her broom and stared straight ahead. Toby hesitated, then clambered on behind. As his feet left land, he was forced to grab onto her cloak. The witch flinched at his touch, and Toby cringed. He had no choice though. If he didn't hold on tight, he'd be plastered to the ground in no time.

To make matters worse, they joined the line alongside Skylark. If it weren't for Toby, it was highly likely she wouldn't be sitting here today. It was highly likely she wouldn't even be alive. But it seemed she was as arrogant as ever, and she, too, ignored him. She might have the beauty of a swan, but she had the warmth and friendliness of a glacier.

Why on earth had he come?

Behind Skylark sat her younger sister, Witch Daisy. She gave a timid wave. "Hi, Toby."

"Daisy! How are you?"

"Good, thank you. I turned nine last week."

"Happy birthday!"

"In a year, I get to make my own wand." Daisy's cheeks flushed with excitement.

A spark of happiness flickered through Toby. He may have lost his house, but he had rescued Daisy, as well as Skylark, from the SMI. Now she had the chance to grow up, to make a wand.

"Ready to depart?" called Witch Willow from the head of the procession.

Bumble twisted round to grin at Toby. "Off to the wizards!"

Toby couldn't help but smile back. She may be annoying at times, but her enthusiasm was infectious.

A pack of large dogs with wings hovered in the air above them. One of them swooped down and nuzzled Toby's arm. Cuddles, Bumble's Golden Retrieagle.

"Hey, boy." Toby stroked his ears.

39

Maybe this holiday would be OK after all.

"Proceed for Wildhaven!" Willow cried.

The line surged forwards and through the entrance hall. As they popped out into the sky, the witches in front disappeared in invisible bubbles. Flame-Red flicked her wand and muttered the words Toby had come to know well:

> *Grow me a bubble*
> *Let me not be seen*
> *Keep me from trouble*
> *With invisible screen.*

The air around them took on a hazy quality, and once more, they could see the line of witches stretching before them.

Almost immediately, they hit a headlong gust of wind, and Flame-Red's mass of coarse curls smacked Toby in the face. He'd left his mouth ajar, and the wiry hairs tickled the back of his throat. He spat them out and clamped his lips together.

They flew for hours, surrounded by white, swirling clouds. How did the witches know where they were going? Every so often, Toby glimpsed the land below. It changed from towns and villages to wild moors and rugged hills, an expanse of green and brown.

Eventually, he started to slump with exhaustion. His limbs ached, but he couldn't adjust position in case he lost balance. They seemed to be travelling north. It was getting cooler, especially this high. Toby snuggled deeper into his jumper. No wonder the witches wore thick cloaks.

In front, Bumble's broomstick was rocking – she

was evidently tiring of the journey too. She leant heavily to one side and began to slip round the broom.

"Bumble!" screamed Toby and Flame-Red in unison.

Bumble gave a start and righted herself. Barnaby shot out of her pocket and landed on her shoulder. From then on, whenever her body sagged, the bat bit her ear, and Bumble jerked awake. Toby made a mental note never to travel on her broom again.

The next time the clouds parted, a vast sea stretched beneath. The front of the procession veered to the left, and there was Willow leading the way, sitting confidently and regally. They were losing height too, and a cluster of islands became visible below. The line dipped lower and lower as the witches steered their broomsticks down.

So that was where they were heading.

One by one, the witches alighted on a short stretch of sand on the northernmost island. Flame-Red sprang deftly off her broom, but Toby's wobbly sky legs gave way beneath him, and he collapsed onto the beach. As he tried to stand, an incoming wave caught him unawares, foaming around his ankles and soaking his trousers.

Flame-Red let out a snort of laughter.

Toby glared back.

He squeezed the seawater from his trousers and splashed further up the beach. The witches stood silently in huddles. *Why were they so quiet?* The buoyant mood that had infected them at the start of the trip had vanished. Instead, puzzled, even concerned, expressions rested on several faces.

Mutterings came from all around: "Where are they?"
"They're always here!"
"Something must have happened."
What was going on?

CHAPTER SEVEN

Toby squelched over to Bumble, his feet becoming heavier with each step as sand glued itself to his wet shoes. She stood with Witch Wing. By their side, Cuddles, the bird-dog, sat with his tail drooping.

"Is something the matter?" Toby asked as he tried to shake his feet clean.

"Well…" Bumble's eyes roamed the beach. "The wizards are supposed to be here to meet us."

"Maybe they got the date wrong?"

"But they've never got it wrong! Not once in all these years," burst out the witch. "We visit Wildhaven on the first day of the new moon in August. They should be here burning a big fire, roasting lectilites and gringles."

Oh great, thought Toby, *more disgusting wyline food.*

Bumble pulled the warbler from her neck. "I knew it was strange Wizard Merrycheeks wasn't replying to me." She held the tip of her wand to the disc and squinted into it. "Hello? Hello? Merry – can you hear me?" Her face fell. "Nothing."

"Witches!" came Willow's voice. The clan gathered around their leader, their bodies tense. "I know you're all concerned at the lack of greeting party, but I'm sure there is nothing to worry about." She held her wand outstretched, and although she spoke softly, her words travelled to every member of the group. "So let's enter the caves and rouse those lazy wizards!"

A few witches gave a half-hearted chuckle, but it was clear none of them were convinced.

"Still, for safety's sake," continued Willow, "please keep quiet and be prepared for flight at a moment's notice. Positions, please!"

Once again, the witches formed their two by two procession, each tightly clasping their wand. After a moment of hesitation, Toby squeezed in beside Flame-Red. With no proper place, he stuck out like a splinter on a broom.

The beach was cut off from the rest of the island by a sheer and impenetrable cliff. There was no way out. Willow led them alongside the rock face, the line of witches snaking across the sand behind her.

As the front of the queue passed a patch of brown seaweed, it rustled and crackled.

"Uh oh," said Bumble.

The seaweed slithered towards the witches, rearing like a snake ready to strike.

"Serpent! Serpent!" shrieked Bumble.

Willow and several other witches raised their wands, and a jet of fire streamed towards the seaweed. It disintegrated in a puff of black smoke.

Mutterings went down the line:

"… Security measures …"

"… Why haven't the wizards removed them …"

They were about to move forwards once more when

the cliff rumbled. Toby looked up to see the whole thing shaking and clods of soil hurtling towards them. The clods rolled over and over, gathering earth as they went and growing bigger with each turn. Every single witch seized their skirts and ran towards the sea. Toby raced after them.

Now the size of footballs, the clumps of soil bounced off the bottom of the cliff and careered after Toby and the witches, hot on their heels. Near the shore, jagged rocks jutted out of the ground. Everyone scrambled onto them just as the football-sized soil caught up. It bounced past, hitting the water with a tremendous splash.

"Mercy me." Bumble clasped a hand to her chest.

Toby wiped his brow. This was the first day of the holiday, and he'd almost died for the third time. Before he could catch his breath, a clattering came from amongst the rocks, like someone's teeth chattering. Hundreds of white clam shells were emerging from the crevices. They crawled towards the witches, opening and closing like sets of jaws.

Willow lifted her wand:

Stop your attack
We are not bait
Return to your
Former shell state.

Every witch followed suit, and the chant rang around the beach. The spell pinged off the clams with small sparks but didn't halt them.

"That one has a toe in it!" shrieked Bumble, pointing at one.

"I'm sure it's not a toe," Wing said, trying to keep the shells at bay.

"It is! It's a toe!"

Toby stepped backwards only to find the clams behind him too. He was completely surrounded. One grasped the end of his trainer and clung on, its sharp edge digging into his flesh. He kicked and shook his leg, but the clam wouldn't let go. *Great.* He was going to lose a toe.

Bumble waved her wand frantically at any shell in sight.

> *Stop your attack*
> *I am not foe*
> *Please keep away*
> *From my big toe.*

The clams continued advancing. They snapped at her boots, and she hopped from one foot to the other. As she did so, she kicked a shower of sand into the nearest one. It choked and gasped, and with a groan, its two halves fell apart and lay motionless on the beach.

"Sand! Sprinkle sand in them," cried Wing.

All around, witches threw sand into the shells, and with coughs and moans, the clams grew still. All except the one attached to Toby, which was clamped tightly to his foot.

With a sigh, Flame-Red walked over, grabbed hold of it and pulled. It gripped Toby's shoe even harder. He winced, trying not to cry out in pain. He wasn't going to lose *one* toe; he was going to lose all five. He'd never play football again.

Daisy rushed over with a seagull feather and tickled the shell. It opened a crack, and she inserted the tip.

With an "*A...A...Achoooooo!*" the clam opened wide, spat out the feather and shot backwards.

Flame-Red threw sand into it, and with one last splutter, it broke in two. She stalked off.

"Um… thanks," said Toby, massaging his foot.

"Welcome," said Daisy. "You saved me; now I've saved you." She gave a shy smile before hurrying off to Skylark.

The witches reformed their procession and made their way up the beach. Toby limped along, avoiding every shell, stone and seaweed and anything else that might suddenly come alive.

They reached the cliff without further incident, and Willow stopped at a narrow crevice. She held her wand aloft:

Open wide
Let us past
Only close
After the last.

There was a creaking noise, and the rock slid apart, leaving a hole several feet across. Willow peered inside, and her voice travelled back along the procession. "The lanterns are not on. Please light your wands."

"The security measures on, but the lanterns off? What is going on?" Bumble half wailed, half whispered.

Witch Wing shot her a frown, and Bumble bit her lip.

As the line moved forward, Toby hesitated. Should

he follow the witches through this unknown hole? He didn't have many options. If he stayed on the beach alone, he could be stranded forever. And who knew what other horrors lay in wait?

As each witch entered the opening in the cliff, they muttered:

Shine me a beam
Let there be light
In this darkness
Give me sight.

Toby passed through the hole into a damp, cold tunnel. *What an awful place to live.* It made his small, tired house seem luxurious.

Slime dripped down the walls, and a drop of water plopped onto Bumble's head.

She gave a little shriek. "What is happening? The wizards always keep this place so cosy!"

Wing silenced her with a nudge of her elbow.

Their footsteps trudged softly on the sandy floor. And the dim rays conjured by the wands bobbed on the rock walls, leaving eerie shadows to dance in dark corners.

The tunnel twisted and turned, gradually climbing deeper into the cliff. Eventually, Toby emerged into a large, central cave. Shafts of natural light filtered down from openings in the roof. The stale salt air was fresher here, but there was a strange smell, and it wasn't pleasant. What was it? Rotten vegetables? Mouldy fruit?

The witches gasped as they took in the scene before them. Broken chairs and tables were strewn across the ground, and discarded belongings lay scattered around. Here a book, there a striped handkerchief, and over on the left, even a worn boot. And what was that lying against the far wall? It couldn't be ... could it? *Surely not.*

Next to Toby, Flame-Red stiffened.

Bumble's hand flew to her mouth.

An ominous silence fell.

"Witch Eagle?" summoned Willow.

A witch with sharp, piercing eyes and feathers entwined in her hair stepped from the crowd. She was dressed from head to toe in silver uniform.

"If you may." Willow motioned towards the wall.

Tentatively, wand outstretched, Witch Eagle crept forwards. As she neared the bundle, she made a retching sound and covered her nose. With her wand, she poked the black cloak. It didn't move. The witch hurried back to the clan; her face said it all.

CHAPTER EIGHT

Witch Eagle's eyes searched the group till they rested on a stout witch. "I'm sorry, Witch Ash – it's Wizard Shield."

The place exploded with shrieks.

Toby's stomach did a somersault. He was in a dank, gloomy cave with a dead body.

The colour drained from Flame-Red's cheeks, Daisy wrapped herself in Skylark's cloak, and Bumble quivered so much she was on the verge of toppling over.

Witch Ash let out an animal wail. Her knees buckled, and she collapsed to the floor, convulsed with sobs.

"Take her back down the tunnel," said Willow gravely.

The distraught witch fought off her helpers, lashing out uncontrollably. But as her energy ebbed, she allowed herself to be half carried, half supported towards the tunnel entrance.

"All witchettes under the age of twelve and their mothers, please follow them," commanded Willow. Despite the situation, she seemed as composed as ever. "Stop at the end of the tunnel, do not exit onto the beach."

The crowd pulsed with panic as witches clutched

their children.

"Orderly fashion! Stay calm."

Half the clan remained in the central cave, faces pale, arms wrapped round one another. Toby shifted awkwardly from one foot to the other, alone in a sea of dark cloaks. It didn't feel right to be here. This was the witches' tragedy, not his.

"Silver Keepers!" called Willow.

Five witches wearing silver uniforms joined Witch Eagle in front of the Head Witch. *Silver Keepers* – the witches who helped keep order in Little Witchery.

"Please investigate the wizards' quarters," said Willow.

The Silver Keepers picked their way around broken bottles and smashed plates splattered with the remnants of an old meal. Reaching three doors in the rocky wall, they split into twos, and each pair crept cautiously through an entrance.

For the next twenty minutes, the waiting witches said very little.

At one point, Toby whispered, "What do you think happened?"

Flame-Red only shrugged, bewilderment and fear on her face.

She edged over to Willow. "Mum?"

"Not now, Flame! Can't you see I have things to deal with?"

Flame-Red's shoulders drooped, and she dropped back.

Bumble shot a look at Wizard Shield's body and sniffed noisily. She tore a purple patch from her dress and blew her nose. The patch regrew, and Bumble let out a yelp. Nestled amongst the bright red, yellow, blue, purple, and green patches was a new black one. Bumble ripped it off, and it grew back black again. "Sizzling serpents," she muttered.

When the Silver Keepers returned, Witch Eagle clutched a sandy-coloured furry animal with large, pointed ears and a bushy tail.

"Marvin!" Flame-Red rushed forwards and grabbed the creature. Quivering, it nuzzled into her chest. "My brother would never leave you behind. What happened?"

"The place is completely empty," said Eagle. "There's more scenes of destruction but no wizards anywhere."

"It's clearly not safe for us to remain," came Willow's voice.

Toby made a move for the tunnel. The sooner they left, the better.

"But before we depart," continued Willow, "let us look for mice."

At once, the witches began to hunt around the cave.

"Here, mousey mousey. Here, mousey mousey," murmured Bumble, peering amongst the rubble with the glow from her wand.

What the…? The witches had always been bonkers, but this was ridiculous. What on earth did they want mice for?

"Found one!" Bumble exclaimed.

The witches paused to watch.

She waved her wand, there was a spark, and the mouse squeaked and scurried off. "Oops! Sorry," she said. "A real one."

The hunt resumed. Flame-Red put Marvin on the

floor, and he sniffed around, close to her legs.

What was he? He was like a fox, though smaller and the wrong colour. And with those ears, he seemed half bat.

Feeling like a spare part, Toby started to lift stones and peek underneath. Better to be bonkers and join in than look silly standing by yourself, right?

The witches searched the cave thoroughly, though no one went near the body of Wizard Shield and the pungent stench around it.

Just as Willow began to suggest there weren't any mice to be found, Witch Eagle cried: "Over here! Under this box."

Willow held out her wand:

> *Are you mouse*
> *Or are you foe?*
> *Reveal yourself*
> *From head to toe.*

There was a spark, and suddenly a full-sized man stood in front of Willow, the box balancing on his head.

Toby jumped backwards, knocking into a witch behind him.

"The wizards turn attackers into mice," whispered Bumble.

Now she told him?

The man threw the box to the ground. Before he could move, Willow waved her wand again, and he shrank to the size of a squirrel. As he started to scamper away, Flame-Red dived to the floor and grabbed him.

The man squirmed and wriggled in her grasp.

"I suggest you cooperate." Willow's voice rang out again. "Unless you wish to stay as a mouse in this cave for the rest of your life?"

Flame-Red deposited him on a table where he stood, fists clenched.

"Thank you, Flame. Rather unsophisticated, though. Do remember your spells," said her mum. "And you are?" she asked the man.

No reply.

"Um... He's wearing camouflage clothes," said Toby. "I think he's from the army."

Willow's eyes narrowed. "I see."

The man was missing one of his boots, and his foot was wrapped in bandages smeared with dried blood. Toby thought of the toe which Bumble had seen in one of the clams. Thank goodness his own toes were still intact.

"What are you doing here?" Willow tried again.

Silence.

"As I said, I have no qualms leaving you here as a mouse if that's what you wish."

"With a hungry whiskertail for company," added Flame-Red wickedly, picking up the fox-thing.

"There is no need for that, Flame," said Willow.

Flame-Red glowered at her feet.

"I will repeat my question only once." Willow directed her wand straight at the soldier. "What are you doing here?"

"On deployment. To capture a hostile force at this location," he said through gritted teeth.

Angry murmurs reverberated through the clan:

"Hostile force?"

"How dare he!"

Willow pursed her lips. "And why were you to capture the wizards?"

"Orders. We were told they were a threat." He indicated Willow's raised wand. "As are you."

"We're not the ones who kill!" shouted an enraged witch from the crowd.

"Earthens!" hissed another.

The hairs on Toby's back prickled. Was he in as much danger as the man?

Bumble placed a protective arm around his shoulders. "Don't worry. They're not talking about you."

For once, he didn't shrug her off.

"Who gave you this order?" asked Willow.

"My sergeant," replied the soldier.

"What has happened to the wizards?"

"No comment."

Flame-Red put Marvin on the table. At the sight of the mini man, the fox's nose twitched, and it licked its lips.

"Flame!" said Willow.

The soldier's eyes flitted to the fox. "I don't know! I heard mention of somewhere called Brocklehurst … near Oxford … but that's all. It was a top-secret mission."

Willow scooped up the small box and waved her wand. Air holes appeared in its lid. They were singed around the edges, and one gave off a tiny plume of smoke. The Head Witch never normally made mistakes. Despite her calm exterior, it was obvious a storm raged inside.

She shoved the mini soldier unceremoniously into the box. "If you continue to cooperate with us, I will return you to your original size and release you when the time comes." She shut the lid firmly, tying it with several strands of her hair.

Willow turned to the witches. "It's late, and I know you must be tired and hungry. We'll head to a safe spot inland to spend the night. Keep brave, Sisters. Tomorrow, we'll decide our plan of action."

CHAPTER NINE

Toby unrolled his sleeping bag on the grass. Nearby, Flame-Red stood stroking Marvin.

"Is that a fox?" asked Toby.

Flame-Red regarded him suspiciously.

"Back home, they're red, and they don't have those massive ears."

"It's a whiskertail," said Flame-Red.

Toby raised his eyebrows. *Another made-up witch word.*

"He's from the Sahara Desert. Witch Wool found him as an abandoned cub when she was hunting for camel fur. For yarn for her shop. She gave him to my brother, Tally." Flame-Red gave a noisy sniff. "Tally doesn't go anywhere without Marvin. Something really terrible must have happened."

Toby shifted awkwardly. "I'm sure your brother will be all right." He regretted the words as soon as they left his mouth. That was a terrible answer, but feelings weren't exactly his strong point.

"All right? All right!" Flame-Red exploded. "Wildhaven has been turned upside down, Wizard Shield is dead, the rest of the wizards are missing, and you think they'll be all right? I might never see Tally or my father again."

Envy rippled through Toby. He gritted his teeth. He couldn't react each time someone mentioned their dad. Pretty much everyone he knew had a father.

"Who knows what you Earthens will do to my family," continued Flame-Red.

"We're not all bad!" said Toby. "I rescued Skylark last year, remember. But then she went and destroyed the SMI, and now my mum doesn't get any pay. So you witches aren't that great either."

"If she hadn't done it, they'd still be capturing witches!" Flame-Red yelled.

They glared at each other, fists clenched by their sides.

Eventually, Toby turned away.

His stomach rumbled. Supper had left him hungry even though Willow had produced magic beans on toast especially for him.

He reached into his backpack for the apple he'd brought, and a packet of biscuits tumbled out. A note was stuck to them in Mum's handwriting. '*Thought these might come in handy.*'

Legend! She must have got Roger's mum to buy them. She would have used all her energy to write the note too. Toby felt like hugging the biscuits.

Talking of his mum, he'd better text her – she wanted him to keep her up to date. But what on earth could he say? He turned on his phone. No reception. Well, that solved that, then.

Toby bit into one of the biscuits, and the chocolate chips melted on his tongue. He took another big bite.

When he next glanced up, Flame-Red was watching a group of witches her age. She didn't seem to be making any attempt to join them. Instead, she cuddled Marvin, looking lost.

Toby sighed and held out a biscuit. "Here, have this."

She scrutinised it.

"I'm not going to poison you!" he said.

Cautiously, she took the biscuit and nibbled the edge. "Spellsparking!" She crammed more into her mouth. "What are those brown bits?"

"Chocolate."

"Choc…olate." She rolled the word around on her tongue. "Do you get to eat it every day?"

"If you can afford it," replied Toby wryly.

Flame-Red eyed him but didn't push it further. She shivered, wrapping her cloak around her.

"Can't you magic a sleeping bag?" Toby asked.

"We can't make something out of thin air!" said Flame-Red. "And I didn't bring anything. I wasn't exactly expecting to spend the night outside."

"You can make food out of thin air."

"Yes, and it's hardly filling. It's like eating air itself."

So that's why he was still hungry after supper.

"I guess I can make my cloak bigger, though," said Flame-Red.

She glanced around before removing a pouch from her pocket. Opening it, she withdrew a tiny glass bottle which clinked against several others.

Toby peered closer. The label written in black ink read *Enlargio.*

"I prefer potions to spells," said Flame-Red. "Mum doesn't know I've brought them. She wouldn't be pleased. We're not supposed to mess with them outside school." She shot Toby a warning look. "So don't tell anyone, all right?"

Flame-Red spread out her cloak and squeezed two purple drops from the bottle. The material rippled like an inky puddle stirred by a breeze. Slowly it grew, creeping across the grass. Toby shuffled backwards. It was like the cloak was alive. Exactly how good – or bad – was Flame-Red at potions? Should he start running? Once the cloak was almost twice its size, it stopped and lay motionless on the ground. Toby touched it with the tip of his toe. It was lifeless once more.

Flame-Red picked the cloak up and draped it around her shoulders. She spun on the spot until she resembled a caterpillar in a cocoon. Then she plopped onto the floor.

Toby snuggled into his sleeping bag and pulled the hood over his head. "Mmm, this is SO comfy."

Flame-Red glared at him and rolled onto her side, facing away.

Back to the grumpy lion.

It took Toby ages to fall asleep. Bumble's snores were loud enough to wake the dead. At the edge of camp, several witches kept guard, little lights glowing at the end of their wands.

Barnaby flitted through the sky, a tiny silhouette against the moonlight, and Toby watched until his eyelids grew heavy.

Just before he dropped off, Willow's words popped into his mind: '*Tomorrow, we'll decide our plan of action.*'

Oh, heck. What was she going to do now?

CHAPTER TEN

Dawn light filtered through Toby's eyelids, waking him far too early the next morning. Dozens of seagulls wheeled and cackled overhead, and he burrowed into his sleeping bag, trying to shut out the din.

He was really warm. Surprisingly warm, considering how misty it was. He rolled over to find a large golden mass pressed against his side. *Cuddles!* No wonder he was hot. Toby trailed his fingers through the bird-dog's fur, and Cuddles grunted with contentment. He wriggled around on his back, got to his feet and gave an almighty shake. Clouds of golden hair flew into the air.

"A…A…Achoo!" sneezed Bumble. "Go to sleep, Cuddles," she muttered. "It's far too early."

The Golden Retrieagle stretched his magnificent eagle wings and flapped high into the air, then soared downwards, pouncing on Toby.

"Gerroff," he laughed, throwing out his arms in defence.

Cuddles batted Toby playfully with his paws.

"OK! OK. I'm getting up."

Most of the witches were still asleep, black-cloaked mounds dotted across the hillside. Witch Willow and the six Silver Keepers were already awake. They sat in a circle, deep in conversation.

Bleary-eyed, Toby stumbled over to a nearby brook. He scooped up the cool water, washing his face and drinking thirstily. As he headed back, Willow beckoned him over.

"Toby," she began, "you helped us so much by rescuing Skylark. We are forever in your debt."

He groaned inwardly. He knew what was coming next.

She paused. "But may I ask – have you heard of this Brocklehurst? Near Oxford, the soldier said."

"Nope. Don't know it. Can't help, I'm afraid," he said hurriedly.

Willow nodded. "We've come to a decision. I'm going to send the clan home. However, I myself and two Silver Keepers intend to find out what's happencd to thc wizards. We'll start by looking for Brocklehurst. I was wondering…"

Toby's stomach sank.

"…I was wondering if you would join us," Willow finished.

"You do realise you're against the army!" exclaimed Toby. "You could get arrested … or shot. More to the point, *I* could get arrested or shot."

"I understand," replied Willow. "We'll only be looking. You won't have to do anything. Unfortunately, the mini soldier can't help us. He escaped during the night." Her eyes roamed the valley. "Foolish man. He's half the size of a whiskertail. He'll be stuck forever on this island. Without him, we have no idea of what we're heading into. So your knowledge of Earthens could prove invaluable."

Here we go again. She was dragging him into yet another escapade. "I'm sorry. I can't help," he said. "I can't get into any more trouble. My mum would never cope. Can you take me home, please?"

"Your mum's happy in the knowledge you're having a holiday," said Willow. "Are you sure it would be a good idea to return home so soon? Won't it cause her more stress?"

That was unfair, but she did have a point. "If I come, I'm not going to get involved with anything."

"Thank you, Toby."

"Wait!" He hadn't actually agreed to help, but the Head Witch was already striding away.

Toby ran after her. Maybe now would be a good time to ask her about creating money by magic. If he was doing something for her, then it went both ways, didn't it? "Willow! Um … you know how after Skylark destroyed the SMI, my mum stopped getting paid?" The words caught in his throat. This was hard to say, but he needed to be quick – more witches were waking and shaking out their cloaks. "I was wondering…"

Flame-Red marched over to them. "What's going on?"

Toby shut his mouth abruptly.

"I'm about to make an announcement to everyone," replied Willow.

"You're going to look for the wizards, aren't you?" said her daughter.

"A few of us are, yes. Toby will accompany us."

"I'll come too."

"No, Flame," said Willow.

"But where will Toby ride? Wouldn't having an Earthen clinging to you rather cramp your Head Witch style? And I can't see any of the Silver Keepers being happy with one on their broom, either. I'll take him."

Willow gave her a pointed stare. "Don't argue with me. You'll return to Little Witchery with the rest of the clan."

"Mum, you promised Toby a holiday. He should at least have someone of his age for company."

Toby raised his eyebrows. *Now* Flame-Red wanted to be friendly with him? How very convenient.

Willow sighed. "All right. You can come. But only as a chauffeur. You will not be involved in any investigations."

The young witches whom Flame-Red had been watching the previous evening strolled past. "Mummy's little darling," muttered one, flicking her glossy black tresses over her shoulder. Ebonia's daughter. What was her name? Her bright green eyes locked with Flame-Red's, and then she stalked off. *Gemeralda*. That was it.

Flame-Red scowled.

Bumble came over and patted her arm. "Don't worry yourself about that one. You know your mums are opponents." She turned to Toby. "Chip off the old wand is Gemeralda. Does whatever Ebonia tells her. Best you stay away."

"Ah, Bumble. I see you've joined us," said Willow. "I'm going to make an announcement."

"Ooh, what about?" said Bumble.

"If everyone would just wait one moment, we'd get along a lot faster," said Willow.

"If Toby's going somewhere, I'm going too."

Willow grimaced. "You're not invited. A few of us are setting out to find the wizards. A small party only."

Bumble put her hands on her hips. "I consider myself his guardian. I brought him into this bubbling cauldron of a mess in the first place. And I vowed to myself that I'd protect him."

Toby gave a weak smile. It was sweet of her, but if he were to choose somebody to 'protect' him, Bumble wouldn't be near the top of the list. She wasn't exactly the best at magic.

"No, Bumble," Willow said.

"Yes."

"No."

"Yes."

Toby looked back and forth between them so many times, he grew dizzy.

Eventually, Willow relented. "You can come but not your animals. That goes for you, too, Flame."

Bumble put a hand over Barnaby in her pocket, and Flame-Red gripped Marvin tighter in her arms. The two witches exchanged glances.

"And make sure you stay discreet, all right?" continued Willow.

Toby resisted the urge to laugh. *Bumble? Discreet?* This was going to be a disaster.

The clan gathered around Willow as she explained the plan once more.

Faces creased with worry.

"Shouldn't more of us come?"

"They've got my son."

"My father!"

"My brother!"

The cries echoed round the group.

Willow raised her arms for silence. "The fewer who go, the less conspicuous we'll be. I'll call for assistance should we need it."

Reluctantly, the witches pulled on cloaks and mounted broomsticks. Gemeralda hung back, darting glances at Willow and Flame-Red. Under her arm, she clutched her bag full of rope. *What was that about?*

Cuddles nudged Toby's leg, and he stroked the bird-dog's ears. "See you again soon, I promise."

Toby stood with Willow, Bumble, Flame-Red, Eagle, and a second Silver Keeper as they watched the procession of witches take to the skies. The clan grew smaller and smaller, the witches' black cloaks billowing like a flock of cravens on the horizon.

"Broomsticks!" called Willow. "To Oxford."

Toby climbed on behind Flame-Red, and they rose into the air. His stomach churned as they picked up pace. He shouldn't have drunk so much water from the brook. And please don't say he needed the toilet already? "Nerves, it's just nerves," he whispered to himself.

Gradually, his tummy settled. Maybe he was actually getting used to this flying business. But then his ears grew hot like someone's eyes were boring into the back of him. Were they being followed? Flying might be getting a bit easier but turning his neck to look was a step too far. It was probably just a bird. He clutched Flame-Red and concentrated on the journey ahead.

CHAPTER ELEVEN

Toby and the witches flew over sea and land, the rolling waves changing to hills and countryside, then villages and cities. They stopped twice to find their bearings, studying buildings and road signs, and finally alighted in an alleyway in a busy town centre. Toby wobbled off the broom, but his legs didn't give way. Yes, he was definitely getting the hang of it.

Willow patted down her hair. "I believe we are in Oxford. It's been a while since I was here."

"I thought you never left Little Witchery?" said Toby.

"Witches used to undertake the occasional trip to keep up-to-date with Earthen affairs. That was when it was safer." She paused. "Now, this is as far as I can get without something to show us where Brocklehurst is. Over to you, Toby."

He sighed. Already he was getting involved. But finding a map shouldn't be too difficult. At the end of the alleyway, he glanced back. With Bumble's multicoloured patchwork dress, Eagle's feather-entwined hair and Willow and Flame-Red's voluminous orange curls, the witches couldn't have stood out more if they'd tried. Then there were the two Silver Keepers' uniforms, which frankly made them look like astronauts waiting to board a space mission. "Stay here. And stay invisible," Toby hissed.

He gave the air a hefty kick, and there was a loud *pop*. That was better. Being in a bubble always made him feel distant from reality – as if he was seeing everything underwater.

The alley led to a high street bustling with shoppers. Toby weaved his way through the crowd, trying to be inconspicuous. Why, then, were so many passers-by staring at him? He passed his reflection in a shop window, and his mouth fell open. On top of his brown hair sat a dazzling blond mohican. *What had Bumble done?* He tried to flatten it, but it sprang up like porcupine spines.

Head down, Toby hurried along the street. Several buildings away on the right was a large bookstore. *Perfect.* A security guard inspected him as he entered, and his eyes followed him all the way up the escalator. Toby took in a deep breath. *You're not doing anything wrong; you're just browsing.*

It wasn't difficult to find a book of maps, and there was Brocklehurst, buried in the countryside north of Oxford. Toby pulled out his phone. It was annoying it didn't have the internet. His friends would have been able to look for the location of Brocklehurst at the touch of a button. But there was no way Toby and his mum could afford a smartphone. At least his mobile had a camera on it.

As he took a photo of the map, a hand grasped his shoulder. "What are you doing, young man? You can't take photos of books."

Toby stuffed his phone into his pocket. "Nothing! Nothing. I'm leaving."

"I suggest you do." The security guard guided him back to the escalator and through the door.

Way to go, Bumble. The man wouldn't have noticed him if it wasn't for the mohican.

Toby rummaged in his bag for his baseball cap and shoved it onto his head. He wasn't going to risk getting the witches to try and fix his hair. If he cut it short as soon as he got home, the blond should have grown out by the time school started. He did *not* want to give Dacker another excuse to pick on him.

As Toby scurried down the street, Bumble peered round the end of the alleyway. She wasn't even invisible anymore.

He rushed over and pulled her further along the passage. "What are you doing?! At least put down your broom. You stand out like a red Retrieagle." He groaned inwardly – did he really just use one of Bumble's own phrases?

"So many people! So many shops!" Bumble's eyes sparkled.

Willow took Toby's phone and studied the picture of the map. "We follow the river till this church … then we head northwest, past this wood…" She took note of several landmarks before passing the phone back.

"Broomsticks, everyone!"

"Where's Bumble?" said Flame-Red.

Willow snapped her neck round. "What? She was here a moment ago."

"She's not now."

Toby ran to the end of the alley. And there was

Bumble, walking in a trance, her arm outstretched as if reaching to touch something.

She was supposed to be there to look out for him, not the other way round.

The witch approached a man sitting on a bench. By his side sat a Golden Retriever. Toby raced after her. When he got there, Bumble was already crouching down, fondling the dog's ears. The owner watched with an amused expression.

"I didn't know Earthens had Golden Retrieagles," Bumble whispered.

"We don't," Toby hissed. "It doesn't have wings. It's plain retriever – no eagle."

The dog nuzzled Bumble, and she laughed with glee.

Toby grasped her shoulder. "We need to go."

The dog headbutted Bumble for more pats, burrowing into her dress. A disgruntled squeak came from her pocket, and Barnaby's nose popped out. The Golden Retriever licked it.

Uh oh.

With an ear-splitting screech, the bat shot into the sky.

"Argh!" The dog's owner jumped to his feet, flapping his arms.

Bumble hopped on the spot. "Barnaby! Come back!"

The bat hurtled through the air like a tiny rocket.

Soon, the whole of the high street was looking up.

"What is it?" shrieked an elderly woman, waving her umbrella.

"It's going to attack us!" yelled a dad, shielding his toddler.

A teenage boy threw a stone at Barnaby, who

squawked wildly. Hackles raised, he dive-bombed the culprit, rising with a clump of hair in his claws.

Chaos erupted. People screamed and scrambled for their lives.

"He's OK! He's OK!" shouted Toby. But he couldn't blame them. He'd reacted the same way the first time he'd met the bat.

Willow appeared behind Toby. "Bumble! You weren't supposed to bring him." She clutched Bumble firmly by the shoulder and shepherded her down the street.

"Barnaby! I can't leave Barnaby."

"I'll get him," said Willow, her lips set in a tight line.

Toby hurried after them. *So much for a discreet trip.*

They joined the other witches, huddled in the alleyway. Willow waved her wand, and an invisible bubble formed around them.

"I'll be right back." She mounted her broomstick and zoomed above the shops, twisting and turning after Barnaby, who had gone full-on monster. She grabbed him and kept hold as he furiously beat his wings.

"Poor Barnaby," whimpered Bumble. "He's terrified."

"You shouldn't have brought him." Witch Eagle narrowed her sharp eyes.

"He goes everywhere with me."

Flame-Red reached forwards to pat Bumble's arm, and a beige snout and black nose peeked out of her cloak. She hurriedly pushed it down and shot Toby an innocent smile.

Oh great – Flame-Red had brought Marvin too?

Willow landed more heavily than normal and shoved

70

Barnaby into Bumble's hands. "Do *not* let me see him again." She smoothed her cloak. "Now, let us leave this place behind."

They flew over the high street, full of frightened shoppers hiding under benches.

"He's just a friendly fluttermouse," muttered Bumble.

Once they could no longer hear the shouts and screams, Toby breathed a sigh of relief. But if they'd caused that much trouble finding a map, how could they possibly find the wizards without any problems?

CHAPTER TWELVE

Brocklehurst turned out to be tiny. They landed by a fountain in a market square, still in their invisible bubbles. As soon as Toby removed his hands from Flame-Red's waist, her whole body relaxed. Gripping tightly to a stranger wasn't exactly his idea of fun either, but Toby wasn't ready to fly hands-free, even if his balance was getting better.

A few buildings lined the square – a bakery, a Post Office, a pub and a small but posh hotel. The whole village was deserted. *What day was it?* They'd flown to Wildhaven on Saturday. *Had that only been yesterday?* That meant it must be Sunday afternoon in this sleepy place.

"Let us explore," said Willow.

"What exactly are we looking for?" Bumble gazed around.

"Any sign of the wizards."

The witches poked their noses through letterboxes and shop doors. They peered over hedges and through windows, and, at one point, Toby found Bumble whispering into a postbox.

"What are you doing?" he said, pulling her back.

"Such an odd contraption. I thought it might be the door to a hidden lair."

"It's a postbox! We put letters in it."

Bumble suddenly frowned at something behind Toby.

He glanced round.

"I thought I saw a figure." She pointed. "Hiding behind that strange wooden stick."

Toby stared at the telegraph pole. There was no one there.

"What is it anyway?" said Bumble. "All those wires going into the houses. That's not to be trusted. Maybe it could lead us to the wizards."

"It gives us electricity."

"Elec…whatty?"

"Electricity! You know, for our lights and heating," said Toby.

"You Earthens make things so complicated," she mumbled.

After half an hour, they'd roamed every road. There was nothing out of the ordinary to be found. Just lines of stone cottages giving way to rolling fields.

They soon found themselves back at the empty market square. Bumble's stomach rumbled loudly. She wandered over to the bakery window, and her eyes went as large as the iced buns. "Can we have one?"

"Do you have any money?" Toby asked, though he knew the answer.

"Noooo," she replied wistfully.

The cakes looked so tasty. Cream oozed out of the chocolate eclairs, and the sugary doughnuts were bursting with jam. Toby's mouth watered. He was invisible …

maybe he could just nip in, slip one off the shelf? *No!* He would *not* steal again.

"Can you magic some money?" He knew Bumble's answer to this, too; he'd asked so many times before.

Willow appeared by his side, making him jump. "I'm afraid we can't do that."

Toby took a deep breath. This wasn't the best moment to bring it up, with Flame-Red and the two Silver Keepers nearby, but it might be his one chance. "Why not?"

"There is no need for witches to have Earthen currency," said Willow.

Toby lowered his voice. "I know, but … um … I don't have a father, and my mum isn't well enough to earn anything. We can't buy everything we need. Clothes, food…" Heat rose in his cheeks, and he trailed off.

"I'm sorry, Toby; I didn't realise things had become so difficult. But I'm afraid it's wyline protocol not to get involved in Earthen affairs."

A surge of anger swept through Toby. "But it's your fault that we don't have any money! When Skylark destroyed the SMI, my mum lost her pay."

Willow placed a hand on his shoulder, but he shrugged it off. "I'm afraid we can't simply create new money. It would interfere with the Earthen economy. We can help in other ways though. We can provide wyline food – nimnuckets, sprugels."

After all he'd done for the witches! Surely a little money for him and Mum wouldn't hurt? And as for nimnuckets and sprugels. *Yuck.* He'd been eating them all year.

Why was he even helping to find the wizards? He'd

never met them, and he didn't care about them. Toby stomped off along a side street and then another.

"Where are we going?" came Bumble's voice from behind.

He turned to find all five witches following him. *Really?* He couldn't get rid of them if he tried.

Toby marched down several more lanes till he passed the last of the cottages and entered open countryside. Still the witches followed. As he walked, his anger faded from full-blown fury to general grumpiness. It probably wasn't wise to lose them. He was in the middle of nowhere with no way to get home. Unfortunately, he needed the witches as much as they needed him.

Toby climbed over a crumbling wall and leant against the cold stone. Lifting their skirts and grunting, the witches did the same. Bumble plopped next to him. "Did you find something?" she asked, leaning in with a conspiratorial air.

"I just thought I'd take a break."

Willow waved her wand at a pebble which grew to the size of a small boulder. She perched on it gracefully, keeping the bottom of her cloak out of the mud. The Silver Keepers did the same.

"Why don't you enlarge a pebble to sit on, Flame?" said Willow.

Flame-Red mumbled something about spells into her lap.

"It's not difficult," said her mum.

Flame-Red picked at her nails.

Bumble gave a cough. "It's past lunchtime, and I'm as empty as a leaky cauldron. Can we eat?"

Toby was given magic beans on toast again. He was famished, and it only took the edge off his appetite. As they ate, a herd of curious cows wandered over. The witches shrank backwards – apart from Bumble, who reached a hand to the nearest one. It emitted an ear-splitting bellow and shook its head.

"Mercy me!" Bumble grabbed the ends of her dress and scrambled over the wall. The rest of the witches were not far behind.

Laughter built in Toby until he couldn't contain it, and he let out a loud snort. It felt good.

"They're only cows!" he called, but the witches wouldn't come back.

He got up with a sigh and went to join them.

A strong gust of wind came tearing through the valley, flattening the grass. Toby shivered. *Honestly!* He'd been invited on holiday, but here he was, sitting in a field in the middle of nowhere in typical English weather.

Caught by the breeze, a cloud of dandelion seeds puffed into the air. Bumble gave a ginormous sneeze. "Blasted Summer Snizzles." She pulled a yellow patch from her dress to blow her nose, and a black patch grew in its place. Her face fell. "Not again."

Toby whispered, "What's wrong with your dress?"

"I think it knows I'm sad," Bumble replied in a mournful voice. "I thought we'd find the wizards in Brocklehurst, but there's not a cloak or beard in sight."

Flame-Red piped up. "Maybe we should widen the search area? It's not like you could hide several hundred wizards in this tiny village anyway."

Toby's spirits sank. He'd been hoping the hunt

would be called off. "Or maybe they're not here at all."

Bumble scanned the countryside. "This place goes on forever. It'll be like finding a wand in an ocean."

"Witch Eagle, perhaps you can help?" said Willow.

Witch Eagle inclined her head in a small bow. "Certainly." She removed a badge from her dress.

Toby squinted at the picture on it: a bird with large, feathered wings and a yellow beak.

The witch threw the badge into the air. As it soared upwards, it transformed, growing bigger and sprouting wings. Before it dropped towards the ground, the wings opened and beat forcefully. It was a replica of the badge. A brown-bodied, white-headed eagle. But a real, breathing, live one.

Toby watched open-mouthed as the eagle flew into the sky and disappeared from view.

Witch Eagle closed her eyes and placed her fingers either side of her temples.

"She can see what the eagle sees," whispered Bumble.

They sat for so long that Toby grew stiff. He jumped to his feet and stretched his legs. Now would be a perfect opportunity to kick a football around. There was a whole field crying out for it. But he didn't have a ball. And the witches had no idea how to play it. He climbed onto the wall and paced along it like a tightrope.

Willow got to her feet and scrutinised the road. "Did anyone else hear that?"

"What?" asked Flame-Red.

"I keep thinking I hear faint footsteps, like we're being followed."

Weird. Toby had felt someone was following them

on the flight from Wildhaven. Then Bumble had spotted a figure hiding behind the telegraph pole. He peered down the lane, but there was nobody there.

It started to drizzle, and he pulled up his hood.

"Flame-Red!" said Willow sharply.

Marvin's nose was peeking from her cloak, his tongue reaching to catch the raindrops.

"I thought I told you not to bring him?" said Willow.

"I couldn't leave him in Wildhaven by himself," protested Flame-Red.

"Why do you never do what I tell you?" said Willow.

"I do! … Sometimes … But you're never at home, so you wouldn't know."

The engine of a powerful car revved in the distance. It came closer and swept past. Toby stared after it. A black BMW. The car had been too fast to see the driver properly, but it had been a man with fair hair. *Dacker's dad?* Surely not. Lots of people had black BMWs. And what would Mr Dackman be doing out here?

Still cross-legged in a trance, Witch Eagle gave a series of mutterings. "Hmm… Oh… Strange…" Then she went quiet again.

Not long after, the distant beating of wings sounded, and the eagle appeared through the clouds. Witch Eagle opened her eyes and blinked. The bird swooped down, growing smaller and smaller, and by the time it landed in the witch's hand, it was a badge once more.

She pinned it to her dress as the rest of them waited expectantly.

"There is little to see. The fields stretch for miles with no Earthen dwellings. There was one thing, though…"

They all leant forward.

"There's a grassy mound several skytracks away. At first, I thought it was a hill, but then Baldwin flew lower. It has a hidden door in one side."

A hidden door? Was this where the wizards could be?

Willow reached for her broom. "We should investigate."

Toby's stomach tied itself into a knot. Whatever the grassy mound was, it clearly didn't want to be found. "We can't just go straight up to it!"

"We won't land too close, and we'll approach cautiously," said Willow, already astride her broom.

CHAPTER THIRTEEN

Toby and the witches landed on the edge of a wood near the mound. Witch Eagle was right; it looked more like a dome-shaped building hidden under a layer of grass than a hill. There was a door built into it like she'd said, and the mound was too uniform, too perfect. It must be man-made. Over the door hung a sign, but it was hard to read from this distance.

Just off the road, there was a narrow opening in the wall, and a BMW was parked inside. The BMW that had driven past? Dacker's dad? Toby's mind flitted to the strange man he'd seen on Mr Dackman's drive when he'd lost his football – the man's odd clothes, his fear and the bottle that had seemed to move by itself.

A horrible thought dawned on Toby. Mr Dackman and the SMI weren't involved with the disappearance of the wizards, were they? But the SMI building had been destroyed. All trace of the organisation had gone. Toby had visited Fir Tree Close himself to make sure of it.

He jumped as a large drip of water landed on his head. It was still raining lightly, but the trees were sheltering them. So where had it come from? Another drip hit him. He glanced up to see rain pooling on a leaf above him. The leaf wobbled, and Toby got a faceful of rainwater. Did Flame-Red flick her wand? Had she made that happen? He wiped his cheek with his sleeve, gave his baseball cap a shake and shuffled a few paces to one side.

"It doesn't look like we're going to find out anything from this viewpoint," said Willow. "We should get closer."

"Um, are you sure about that?" Toby's eyes darted again to the BMW. "It might be dangerous."

"We need to see if the wizards are here," said Willow. "We can use Snapback Seeds to keep us safe."

She removed a pouch from her pocket, withdrew three seeds and threw them onto the ground. They wriggled and vibrated before splitting open. Dark green roots and shoots surged out. The roots slithered into the earth, taking hold, while the shoots curled upwards into long, strong vines.

Willow tied one to her waist. "If we get into any trouble, these will snap us back to the woods."

"Like a bungee rope?" said Toby.

The witches all stared at him blankly.

"You jump off a cliff and umm…" he trailed off as their eyes went round.

"Jump off a cliff?" spluttered Bumble. "Why ever would anyone do that?"

With everyone distracted, Flame-Red started to tie one of the vines around her own waist.

"No, Flame!" said Willow. "The Silver Keepers are coming with me. You, Bumble, and Toby are to stay here."

"Let me go! I'm lighter on my feet than you," protested Flame-Red.

Her mum silenced her with a glare.

The three witches crept forwards, pausing every few steps. As they edged closer to the mound, Toby clenched his fists. Surely they'd stop soon? They weren't actually going to try and go into the hill, were they?

A few metres from the door, Willow froze, craning her neck to read the sign above it. She turned to the woods and, face pale, tried to mouth something. Behind her, Witch Eagle took another step. It was then that it happened. One second, Willow and the Silver Keepers were there. The next, a hole had opened in the earth, and they were falling. Their black cloaks flew up around their heads like giant bat wings as they disappeared from sight. There came an ominous pop, pop, pop as each of their invisible bubbles burst, followed by three loud thuds. A metal grille slid over the pit, chopping off the Snapback vines before they could react. The vines shot into the woods, smacking into Toby's legs and sweeping him off his feet.

Bumble ran shrieking from the trees, arms flapping. "Willow!" she wailed. She scurried across the grass and peered into the ground where her fellow witches had vanished, and then the earth beneath her opened, and she, too, disappeared from view. Barnaby hurtled out of the hole and into the overgrowth behind them.

Flame-Red made a move to run, but Toby grabbed her. "No! Don't be stupid."

"My mum! I have to help." Flame-Red struggled, lashing out.

Toby hung on so tight, his fingernails dug into her arm, but he didn't let go.

"You can! But not now." He almost shook her in his

attempt to bring her to her senses.

The witch stopped fighting and stood trembling, her breath coming in short gasps. Toby kept a firm grasp of her shoulder.

The tip of a wand reached out of the metal grille and wrote three quivering letters in the sky: SMI. The letters shimmered in silver before dissolving into tiny particles.

Toby inhaled sharply.

"What?" cried Flame-Red.

"SMI stands for Society for Magical Investigation. It hunts witches." Cold dread washed through Toby. The wizards must be here. But he couldn't face the SMI again. Not after everything that had happened last year. He should have guessed it would be involved. That meant it *had* been Mr Dackman in the BMW.

The wind rustled through the trees, and the faint sound of male voices drifted over.

Toby dropped back. "We have to get out of here."

"I'm not leaving." Flame-Red folded her arms.

"You can return. But right now, we need to get away. The SMI is bound to come looking to see if there's any more witches."

Two figures stepped from the mound – one stocky with brown hair and one taller with fair hair. Toby squinted. The SMI Director and Dacker's dad.

"Mum'll escape," said Flame-Red. "She has a wand, and she's the best at magic."

"The men might have guns. The SMI must be working with the army now. We found a soldier on Wildhaven, remember?"

"G…guns?" Flame-Red's voice shook. "Those Earthen weapons that can kill with one shot?"

Toby nodded grimly.

The Director held up a small, black box. At once, three white sticks flew out of the ground and attached themselves to it.

Was that a wand-thief? Witch Willow had given Toby one to help rescue Skylark last summer. They were precious and rare. Who would have given one to the SMI?

Flame-Red gave a low moan. "Their wands! They're trapped without them."

"Shhh!" hissed Toby.

He was too late. The Director's head jerked up and stared straight in their direction. Thank goodness they were invisible.

"We have to leave. Now!" said Toby.

Flame-Red stayed glued to the spot.

The Director was gesturing towards the woods. He'd definitely heard them.

Toby gave Flame-Red a sharp nudge. "Come on!"

With one last lingering look, she picked up her broom, her face a rigid mask.

"Where's Barnaby gone?" hissed Toby.

"He won't leave Bumble."

Mr Dackman started striding towards them.

Heart pounding in his chest, Toby sprang onto the broom behind Flame-Red, and they took to the air.

CHAPTER FOURTEEN

Flame-Red manoeuvred the broom carefully around the branches so their bubbles didn't burst. As they cleared the tops of the trees, Toby shot a last look behind. From this height, he could see the four witches huddled at the bottom of the pit.

Bumble!

She might annoy him sometimes – OK, a lot of the time – but over the past year, he'd come to care for her. The realisation hit Toby like a surprise punch. This clumsy woman with her patchwork dress and pet bat was his friend. Would he ever see her again? The broom sped up, and Toby grasped on tightly. He couldn't think about this now. He needed to concentrate on keeping himself upright.

It wasn't the smoothest of rides. The drizzle had stopped, but it was still windy. On top of that, Flame-Red's agitation seemed to be having a curious effect on the broom, and it kept giving little jolts and kicks.

They flew over the woods, the branches lush with leaves from all the rain that summer. After a mile, the trees thinned. Flame-Red steered the broom across the road and into a field.

As they dismounted, she wiped her cheeks. Had Flame-Red been crying? Clearly, she hid a softer side behind her grumpy lion exterior.

Toby slumped against a stone wall. An hour ago, they hadn't even found the wizards, and now their party of six was down to two.

Flame-Red paced back and forth, her wild curls bouncing with every step. "What are we going to do?"

"We?" Toby buried his head in his hands. He'd agreed to come to Brocklehurst on the condition he wouldn't get involved. And now look what had happened. "I'm sorry. I can't help."

"But my mum's been captured! And they already have my dad and brother."

There she was, talking about her family again. Flame-Red didn't know how lucky she was … although not for much longer if he didn't help her come up with a solution.

"I can't get into trouble," said Toby. "I have to think of my own mum. But don't you have…"

"Fine!" Flame-Red spat. "I'll do it myself."

"Just wait a moment! Don't you have one of those warbler-thingies that Bumble wears around her neck? You can call Little Witchery and get help."

"You don't get one till you are sixteen."

"OK," replied Toby, trying to stay calm. "You can fly home and get help."

"Not without a warbler."

"Wha…at…t…?"

"You need a warbler to navigate to Little Witchery," said Flame-Red. "Without one, I have no idea where it is."

Toby swallowed. "No idea at all?"

"No!"

His spirits plummeted into his shoes. Until that instant, he'd assumed Flame-Red could get help and he could wash his hands of the whole situation. But it really was just the two of them. He couldn't leave her by herself.

"Well, you can't do anything today anyway," Toby said eventually. "The SMI will be on high alert. Let's make a plan tomorrow."

Flame-Red sat down, but she couldn't keep still. After a few minutes, she was back on her feet. "I'm going to look for water. I'll fill your bottle." She plopped Marvin by Toby's feet. "He's getting too heavy to carry. Keep on an eye on him."

Toby reached out a tentative hand and was greeted with a low growl. He snatched his fingers away.

"He's wary of new people, but he'll be fine once he gets used to you," said Flame-Red. "He's a nightimal, so he'll sleep all day anyway."

"You mean he's nocturnal."

"No, I mean he's a nightimal."

Toby didn't reply. It wasn't worth arguing. She was as stubborn as Bumble.

Clenching the water bottle tightly in her fist, Flame-Red set off, her long black cloak billowing behind her.

Marvin watched her, his ears back and tail curled close to his body.

Toby delved into his bag, pulled out the pack of biscuits and scattered some crumbs on the ground.

The fox gave them a cautious nudge with his nose before gobbling them up. Then he pawed at Toby's leg.

"You can't have any more!" chuckled Toby. "I need

to save them for later."

Marvin gave a little whine and then scrabbled at the earth. He turned round and round and settled into a ball. He was pretty cute, curled up in his den, even if his teeth did look sharp.

Toby turned on his mobile phone, and it pinged almost immediately.

Hope it's going well, love Mum xx

Drat. He still hadn't texted her. He typed a few words, deleted them and tried again.

Sorry, bad reception. Arrived safely. Wizards live in caves on an island! xx

His finger hovered over the send button. Well, it wasn't a lie, and he couldn't tell her what was really going on. She'd get so worried. He pressed send and turned his phone back off.

A few minutes later, Marvin's eyes snapped open. He lifted his snout and sniffed the air.

"What? What is it?"

The fox planted his front legs halfway up the wall and sniffed again.

Panic streaked through Toby. Had the SMI come looking for more witches? He got to his feet and studied the woods they'd flown over. *Nothing*.

Marvin cocked his large ears, and they swivelled in a circle. Shoulders hunched, he slunk across the field.

What had he heard? Probably another fox or mouse. The countryside must be full of creatures.

Marvin started to run, body streamlined as if hunting prey. But he was chasing nothing … except … as he ran, flattened patches of grass appeared before him, as if something invisible was sprinting away.

A film of cold sweat formed under Toby's jumper.

Reaching the far end of the field, Marvin stopped at the wall, yapping. Then, tail swishing, he trotted back to Toby.

"What was it?" Toby's voice trembled.

Marvin gave one last yap and curled up in his previous spot, clearly happy he'd done his job of fending off evil.

As Toby tried to calm his breathing, the fox lifted his head, and rested it on Toby's lap.

"Hey, boy," whispered Toby.

After a giant yawn, Marvin fell quickly asleep.

For the following hour, Toby stayed alert, but there was nothing to be seen and no sound but the noise of birds and wind. By the time Flame-Red returned, he was feeling sheepish. Marvin must have been hunting a rodent, and as for the flattened grass, Toby snorted at himself. He was so worked up he was imagining dangers.

Flame-Red seemed calmer now; the trek across the countryside had worn her out. She shivered and wrapped her cloak around herself. Day had turned to evening, and the temperature was dropping.

"Can't you magic a blanket?" said Toby. She hadn't looked very comfy the previous night.

"I've already told you! You can't make things out of thin air."

Toby surveyed their surroundings. "Could you make one out of grass?"

89

Flame-Red hesitated. "I don't have a potion for that."

"You could do a spell?"

Her cheeks flushed. "I'm not good at spells. Can't you tell I'm a disappointment to my mum, Head Witch, best-at-spells-since-1988."

"I'm sure you're not," said Toby. "I could help."

"An Earthen help with magic?" Flame-Red scoffed.

"I'm only trying to be friendly. You're the one who's cold."

The witch scowled at the ground. "I don't need friends. I'm fine by myself."

Mummy's little darling. Wasn't that what Gemeralda had called Flame-Red while they were at Wildhaven? Was that why she was unfriendly? Because everyone her age was mean to her? It mustn't be easy having your mum as Head Witch.

"Let's gather some grass and see if you can do anything with it," said Toby.

"I can't."

He wandered around, pulling up fistfuls of the meadow and piling them in a heap. "Go on. You might as well try."

With a sigh, the witch held her wand aloft and mumbled:

Entwine this grass
Keep me warm
Make me a mat
Strong in form.

The pile rustled, and the blades wriggled like worms.

90

Then black tendrils of smoke floated upwards. Flame-Red stamped on them, muttering phrases that sounded decidedly darker than the ones Bumble used. A singed mound of mush lay in front of them.

"See. It's no good." Flame-Red turned away.

"It nearly worked! You didn't say the spell with much conviction," said Toby.

"Like *you* would know how to do magic."

Irritation bubbled in Toby. Why was he even trying to help? She could freeze for all he cared. But that wasn't true. He knew what it was like to be bullied. Dacker and his gang had been awful to him in the past. But at least Toby had friends. Roger and Jazz had always stuck by him.

Toby collected more handfuls of grass and made another pile. "Have another go."

"You really don't give up, do you?" said Flame-Red.

"I tell you what," he said. "I won't watch."

Behind him, Flame-Red said the spell once more. Her voice was stronger, the words a little more confident.

Toby turned to find her holding a green blanket. It wasn't perfect: the edges were uneven, and it was neither square nor circular but something in between. Still, the grass had entwined, and not a single blade stuck out. "Brilliant!"

A small smile flitted across Flame-Red's lips. "Would you like one?"

"I'll be all right with my sleeping bag, but thank you."

For a few seconds, they stood awkwardly, then Flame-Red said, "I guess we might as well go to bed."

Toby glanced at the woods. Darkness was falling,

and they were full of eerie shadows. *Just the trees.* "Do you think it's safe here?" He'd been sure the SMI would come looking. Perhaps they'd satisfied themselves with searching the grounds nearest the hill. "Maybe we should spend the night elsewhere."

Flame-Red shook her head. "I'm not going any further away from my mum. I have to rescue her tomorrow."

Marvin was awake now and roaming up and down.

"That's odd," said Flame-Red. "He normally goes off hunting at night." She tickled him under the chin. "I guess this new place is a bit scary for you, isn't it? Or maybe you think we need defending? Good boy, keep an eye out for us."

Toby settled into his sleeping bag. *What an awful day.* The discovery that the SMI was back, and now the witches had been captured too. Did Flame-Red really believe it was going to be so easy to rescue them? She had no idea.

CHAPTER FIFTEEN

Toby lay on the grass as night crept in around them. With a thick layer of cloud blocking the moon and stars, it was almost pitch black. Flame-Red's outline was barely visible just a few metres away. Strange animal noises filled the air, and Toby suppressed a shiver. He'd always hated the dark. *You're in England*, he told himself. No bears, no lions, no tigers. And as for mice and rats, Marvin would protect them from those. Toby huddled down in his sleeping bag and pulled the hood over his head.

He was drifting off to sleep when he snapped awake. What had disturbed him? He lay stock still, listening. At first, there was nothing apart from the sound of the wind and a distant hoot. But then, there came a low growl and a light filtered through his eyelids.

Toby peered over the top of his sleeping bag, and his heart fluttered as if a moth flapped in his chest. Not more than three feet away stood something, or rather, someone. The figure held a torch and a piece of rope. The figure was not Flame-Red – she was lying on her grass blanket.

Hackles raised, Marvin let out another growl.

Without giving himself time to think, Toby sprang

up and dived for the person's legs. They crashed to the ground with a thud. Toby, still half in his sleeping bag, hung on determinedly, feeling for all the world like an oversized slug.

The person thrashed and kicked, and Toby narrowly avoided being walloped in the head. Where was Flame-Red when he needed her?

And then her voice rang through the night. "Drop your wand!"

About time!

But hang on – *wand?* Not a torch, then. *But that meant it was another witch?*

The person continued to lash out, and Toby held on grimly.

"Drop it!" said Flame-Red. "Or I will turn you into a mouse."

"Like you could do that," panted the person. "We all know you're no good at spells."

Flame-Red's cheeks flushed in the light from her wand. "Who says I need a spell? Want to see the potions I've brought?"

As the intruder hesitated, Toby knocked the wand from her hand.

Flame-Red snatched it up and shone the beam in her face. The witch squinted in the sudden glare.

"Gemeralda!" cried Flame-Red. "What in the name of sizzling serpents are you doing here?"

The witch, with her long black locks and dazzling green eyes, stared back defiantly but didn't speak.

Toby sat up, rubbing his ribs. *Ebonia's daughter.* Why hadn't she returned to Little Witchery with the rest of the clan? Her mum had been too poorly to join the trip to Wildhaven – didn't Gemeralda want to be with her?

"How did you get here? Did you follow us?" asked Flame-Red.

The cogs in Toby's brain whirred. Willow had thought she heard footsteps earlier. And Marvin had chased something that afternoon. "She's been spying on us!"

Flame-Red's eyes blazed.

"And she was holding a piece of rope," added Toby. "I think she was about to tie you up."

"Tie me up?" said Flame-Red. "Why would you do that?"

Gemeralda squeezed her lips together.

"If you don't tell us what you were doing, we'll have to tie you up instead," said Flame-Red.

"You can't do that!" Gemeralda blurted out.

"Watch me." Flame-Red turned to Toby. "Where's the rope?"

"It was here somewhere." He bent down, fumbling in the dark. Then looked back up to see Gemeralda creeping across the grass. "She's getting away!"

Flame-Red was on the witch in an instant, her wand pressed against her chest.

Toby's hands closed over the rope, and he passed it to Flame-Red.

"That hurts," said Gemeralda as it was wrapped around her wrists.

Toby chewed his cheek. "Are you sure we should be doing this?" It didn't feel right, tying up a witch.

"She's not to be trusted," said Flame-Red. "Her mum tried to take over as Head Witch from my mum, remember? Who knows what she was planning to do, sneaking around while we were asleep."

Gemeralda writhed in the bindings. "Wait till my mother hears about this!"

"Wait till *my* mother hears you followed us and were spying on us!" Flame-Red pulled the cord tighter.

As the two witches glowered at each other, something caught the corner of Toby's vision, and his head snapped round.

Flashlights.

In the woods across the road. Four of them, bobbing up and down.

Toby nudged Flame-Red's arm, and the breath caught in her throat. "The SMI?" she whispered.

"I think so."

"HERE!" Gemeralda yelled.

Flame-Red and Toby moved so quickly they almost crashed heads. They rugby-tackled Gemeralda to the ground, and Flame-Red threw her hand over the witch's mouth.

"Not another word!" Flame-Red spat, holding the tip of her trembling wand a couple of millimetres from Gemeralda's nose. "If you make one sound, I swear on the wyline oath, I will turn you into a mouse and leave you in this field forever."

"What was that?" came a distant male voice. "I heard something … over the road."

Toby's heart hammered so loudly he was sure they'd be able to hear it in the woods. "Quick! Our things." He crawled through the grass, grabbing his sleeping bag and the blanket.

"Marvin!" hissed Flame-Red. "Come here."

The fox scrambled up her leg and burrowed into her

cloak.

She pushed Gemeralda's broomstick at the witch. "Get on. Now."

With a scowl, Gemeralda slung her leg over the broom.

Flame-Red poked Toby. "Climb on behind."

Toby baulked. Gemeralda was unpredictable. He didn't want to be anywhere near her.

"You need to watch her. I have to concentrate on flying."

Heavy footsteps tramped across the road. With his pounding heart echoing the stamp of the men's boots, Toby sprang on behind Gemeralda.

Flame-Red straddled her own broom in one fluid movement.

The footsteps stopped, and several shadowy figures clambered over the wall.

Flame-Red whipped out her wand and created a giant bubble around the three of them. She was only just in time. Strong flashlights illuminated the field.

"Search the area!" said a harsh male voice.

With Flame-Red holding onto Gemeralda's broom, the three of them shot into the air. The brooms jerked and bucked at the sudden speed, and Toby had visions of swinging upside down like a repeat of his first-ever broomstick lesson. He clung onto Gemeralda, gripped his knees into the broom, and safely avoided disaster.

In front of him, Gemeralda sat rigid and upright, her hands tied behind her back. Toby held his breath, praying she wouldn't shout out again, but she stayed silent. Clearly, she'd believed Flame-Red's threats. When they were only a few metres high, one of the men passed directly beneath them – a gun in his arms.

As they sped away, Toby's thoughts whirled. Why on earth had Gemeralda called to the SMI?

CHAPTER SIXTEEN

As they flew into the night sky, the lights of Brocklehurst twinkled in the distance. Flame-Red kept them behind, zooming through the dark countryside, getting as far away as possible. With every passing minute, Toby's heart rate slowed, and relief flooded his muscles.

That had been close, but they were safe now – for the moment at least.

After twenty minutes, Flame-Red brought the two brooms into land by a lake. She dismounted and rounded on Gemeralda.

"Why the flapping fluttermice did you cry out to the SMI?"

"I didn't know who it was. I was trying to save myself from YOU."

Flame-Red gave an exasperated scream. "They have guns! They were going to capture us." She dragged Gemeralda to a nearby tree and tied her to it. "Who knows what you'll do next."

"Not so tightly," said Toby. "You'll hurt her."

Flame-Red sighed loudly but loosened the cord a little. She brandished Gemeralda's wand in the air. "I'll be keeping this out of your reach." Then she pocketed it in her cloak.

"You won't get away with this," said Gemeralda. "There's powerful magic in my family."

"Yes, and your grandmother is banished to a cloud, so look where that got her."

Toby frowned. "Banished to a cloud?"

"Witch Zazzle, Gemeralda's grandmother, tried to cause an uprising in Little Witchery thirty years ago. My grandparents were on the Wyline Council at the time. Fortunately Zazzle didn't succeed."

Gemeralda scowled. "The Council didn't have the right to banish her! To separate her from her family."

Toby took a step back. No wonder she bore a grudge.

On the banks of the lake stood a small, dilapidated cabin with a missing roof and crumbling walls. He pushed open the door: tangled ivy hung inside like spider webs, and moss covered the stone floor. It wasn't a palace, but it would be better than sleeping rough in a field, and it should shelter them from the wind.

Marvin scampered round the cabin, sniffing at the ground. He started to dig, soil flying in all directions. Seconds later, he emerged with a large, rusty key clamped between his teeth.

Toby gently prised it from his mouth and tried it in the door. *Bingo!* "Good boy, Marvin. At least this will keep us a bit safer."

With the door locked, Toby unravelled his sleeping bag for the second time that night and lay down. The moss was surprisingly bouncy.

Flame-Red spread out her grass blanket and wrapped herself in her cloak while Marvin scampered off. "What do you think those men are going to do to my mum? To

Bumble?" The words caught in the witch's throat.

Toby's thoughts went to last summer – the operating theatre, the vials of witch blood, the bone in the furnace. He couldn't tell Flame-Red. Besides, surely the SMI couldn't be experimenting on witches again? The Society had wanted to replicate magic for themselves, but only witches and wizards with their silver blood could create magic.

"I've no idea," Toby said. He settled down to sleep, but it was a while before he drifted off.

He was woken several hours later by Flame-Red shaking him. He sat up, bleary-eyed. Was it morning already?

"I'm going to the SMI," she said.

"They'll still be on the lookout. We should wait a bit."

"*We?* I thought *you* weren't getting involved."

She was right. He'd said he wouldn't. But there was no way he could leave Bumble and Willow to the mercy of the SMI.

Toby stood up. "I'll come. But we need breakfast first. We haven't had much sleep, and we've not eaten since lunch yesterday. I can't think straight."

"More beans on toast? I'm not sure I can magic it."

Toby screwed up his nose. "I need REAL food. I've got some biscuits left, but we should probably save those for emergencies." He left the cabin and surveyed their surroundings. Fish from the lake? But how would they catch them? And Flame-Red definitely didn't have the patience. Think again. "There must be some blackberries or something."

"Blackberries?" said Flame-Red.

"They taste a bit like tibtabs."

"All right. I'll look as long as it doesn't take too long."

Gemeralda was still tied to a tree, her glossy emerald dress smeared in dirt and tattered at the hem. She glared at Flame-Red as the witch checked the cords were securely fastened. Toby kept his distance. Gemeralda might not have her wand, but there was a threatening glint in her eyes.

Flame-Red and Toby set off across the fields. As they tackled the first wall, Marvin scampered over to them. Soil coated his legs so it seemed as if he was wearing brown socks.

"There you are, you little mischief-maker," said Flame-Red.

They walked until they came upon a patch of white mushrooms sprouting out of the ground.

"These might be edible." Toby nudged one with his toe.

Marvin sniffed them cautiously and retreated.

"Then again," said Toby, "they could be poisonous. We'd better not."

They tramped across several more fields. Cloud hung heavy in the sky, dew soaked the hem of Toby's jeans, and his stomach ached with hunger.

"What about these?" Flame-Red pointed to a bush covered in red berries.

"I've no idea."

"Do you even know where we'll find blackberries?"

"On a bush … I think," Toby muttered.

"So we're scouring the countryside for some sort of

101

bush? This is hopeless."

Marvin bounded towards another hedgerow, balanced on his back paws, and nibbled at something.

Toby went to get a closer look. Sprinkled with dew, small red fruits glistened like jewels. *Raspberries*. Hundreds of plump, juicy raspberries. *Bingo*.

"We can eat these!" he called.

"You're sure?" asked Flame-Red.

"Yep." Toby plucked one from a spiky branch, and it slid off easily. He took a bite. It was a little sharp but refreshing, and so ripe that it practically melted on his tongue. Before he'd even swallowed, he'd popped another one into his mouth.

Flame-Red hung back.

"Try one!"

She glanced at Marvin, whose muzzle had completely disappeared inside the plant. Only his bottom could be seen, its bushy tail wagging as he munched.

Flame-Red picked a raspberry and chewed. "Not bad … Pretty tasty, in fact."

Soon, they were cramming their mouths and filling their empty tummies. Red juice stained Toby's fingers, but he didn't care. He gorged until he couldn't possibly eat any more.

Flame-Red was still munching noisily.

"Slow down! You'll get stomach ache. So will Marvin if he eats any more. And I don't fancy having to deal with squidgy fox poo." Toby pulled Marvin gently out of the bush.

"Fox?" said Flame-Red.

"Or whatever you call it. Whiskertail or something."

She wiped her mouth and surveyed the rest of the

hedgerow. "I guess we better take some for our *prisoner*."

Toby flinched at the word. They were holding a witch captive. Did that make him and Flame-Red as bad as the SMI? "Maybe we should let her go."

"Not unless she tells us what she's doing here."

"Could you at least make her a grass blanket? We have the cabin, but she's stuck outside."

Flame-Red sighed. "All right! All right. I'll magic her a blanket." She removed her cloak and began to fill it with raspberries.

Worry lines creased her forehead. How could he cheer her up?

Despite his groaningly full stomach, Toby threw a raspberry upwards and caught it in his mouth. "Yes!" He punched the air.

A smile twitched on Flame-Red's lips. She threw a berry into the air and missed. Tried again and missed once more.

"Throw it a bit higher," said Toby. "Here, try this one." He threw a raspberry in an arc above her head, and it landed in her mouth. She grinned.

"High five!" Toby held up his palm.

Flame-Red stared at it in confusion.

Toby dropped his hand. Well, that was one way to look stupid. "You're supposed to hit it."

"But why?"

"It's like a celebration … or a congratulations."

"Oh." Flame-Red sounded unimpressed. She threw another raspberry in the air and caught it first time. "High five!" She lifted her palm.

Toby gave it an enthusiastic slap.

Just then, the sun made an unexpected appearance.

The warm rays soaked into Toby's skin, and he took a deep breath as if trying to inhale them. Bathed in sunlight, the whole valley came alive. A robin on the nearby wall puffed out its chest and sang in praise to the skies. Toby felt almost as if he really *was* on holiday.

His thoughts strayed to his mum. It was such a shame she couldn't get out of the house, couldn't see this, couldn't enjoy this. How long was it since she'd had the sun on her skin? *Too long.*

As the clouds swallowed the sun again, a small shadow flitted through the air. It darted towards them, and Toby threw his arms up to shield his face. The creature landed on his ear, hung upside down and nuzzled his cheek.

"Barnaby! You found us."

Flame-Red pointed to the bat's back. "What's that?"

Something purple was tied around his waist. Toby unravelled it: A square of fabric with frayed edges – a patch from Bumble's dress?

A ring with a large red stone toppled out.

Flame-Red pounced on it. "My mum's ring!"

She rubbed the stone with her forefinger, and a coloured vapour floated out.

With a startled squeak, Barnaby shot into the sky and disappeared.

The hazy particles joined to form a tiny image of Willow, like a genie from a lamp.

Toby gaped at it.

"We are trapped in dungeons," said Genie-Willow, her voice sounding ghoulish. "The wizards are here too. Summon help from Little Witchery."

"We would if we could," muttered Toby, unable to

draw his eyes away from the flickering mirage.

The image disintegrated into sparks which fell to earth like the sputtering remains of a firework.

"She doesn't think I can rescue them myself!" said Flame-Red. "I told you she thinks I'm hopeless."

"She's probably trying to protect you. The SMI is dangerous. Of course she doesn't want you facing them alone."

"I'll show her." Flame-Red spun on her heel and marched off across the fields.

With a groan, Toby picked up the bundle of raspberries and hurried after her.

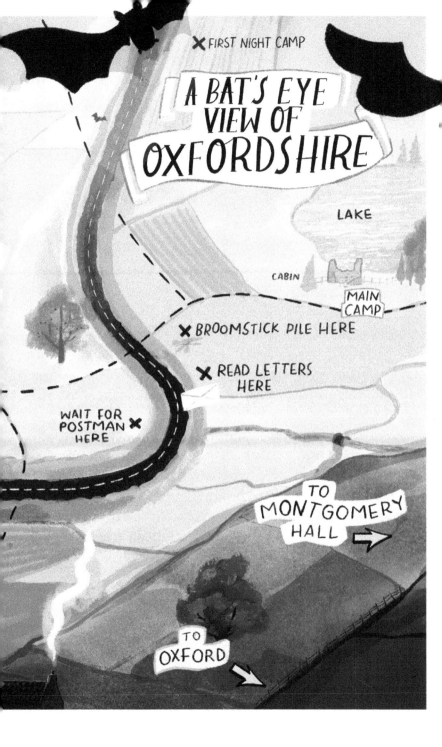

CHAPTER SEVENTEEN

Back at camp, Gemeralda had managed to free one of her hands. Busy fumbling with a strange object, she didn't notice them approaching.

Flame-Red threw herself at the witch, grabbed the object and flung it to the ground. "A flare! Where did you get that?"

Toby eyed the small rocket-shaped object. "Um, something's happening," he said as smoke puffed out of the end.

Before they could do anything, the flare streaked across the grass, leaving a singed path in its wake. It careered onto the lake, skimming the surface like a steam train on skates. A vapour of mist rose from the water in the trail of the smouldering rocket. With a bang, it struck the opposite bank and exploded in a little shower of green.

"Green!" said Flame-Red. "That's your mum's colour. Why are you summoning her?"

Gemeralda didn't reply.

"We've tied her up. I'm not surprised she's calling for help," said Toby.

"But isn't her mum in Little Witchery? And she can't know anyone on Earth. There's no one to call."

While Flame-Red swung her arms around in exasperation, Gemeralda was intent on freeing her other hand from its ties.

Toby pointed at the tree. "You're about to lose her."

With a lion growl, Flame-Red pounced on Gemeralda and resecured her wrists. Then she pulled the belt from her trousers and wrapped it round too. "There. That should prevent you from any further tricks."

"You won't get away with this," spat Gemeralda. "You'll see. Now the SMI has your mum there's nothing you can do about it."

"Want to bet?" Flame-Red grabbed her broomstick and turned to Toby. "Are you coming or not?"

Toby sighed. Here he was, flying straight into danger again.

He dropped a handful of raspberries into Gemeralda's lap and climbed onto the broom.

"Coming?" he asked Marvin.

But full of fruit and a night of wandering, the fox was already curled in a ball asleep.

"I told you, he's a nightimal," said Flame-Red. "He'll sleep all day."

As they flew over fields and hedges, Toby tried to remove his hands from Flame-Red's waist. He wobbled, righted himself, wobbled again and threw his arms back around her. Not this time, but practice makes perfect, right?

Reaching the woods, there was no sign of last night's search party, so they landed in the same spot as yesterday – the spot from which they'd seen Willow and Bumble disappear into the ground.

"We need to find the dungeons my mum

mentioned," said Flame-Red.

"You can't go rushing in. Let's watch for a bit – find out if anyone's around," replied Toby. He was going to have to put her on a leash at this rate.

With thick cloud overhead, murky shadows filled the woods. The wind rustled the trees and whipped down Toby's collar. He shivered.

The Director stepped out of the front door, and Toby inched backwards, even though he was in an invisible bubble. The man walked to and fro, talking animatedly. Flame-Red and Toby strained to hear, but his words were lost in the breeze. Then, a female voice called "JB!" from the door.

Was that someone Toby had heard before? It was too far away to tell.

As the Director returned into the hill, Barnaby flapped round the side. He flew towards the trees before weaving behind the mound and out of sight.

"He wants us to follow him!" said Flame-Red.

Toby groaned. Going any closer to the building was like flying directly into a dragon's lair. But they weren't going to discover much standing here.

Flame-Red was already picking up her broom. "Coming?"

Toby hesitated. "OK, OK. But don't touch the floor. It's probably covered in traps."

They flew cautiously towards the mound, following the route Barnaby had taken. The side near the woods was completely covered in grass, but around the back, they found a window at ground level every few metres. Each was covered with iron bars and open to the elements.

Flame-Red stopped the broom by the first window.

Toby peered in: a barren room with moisture trickling down its stone walls. In the feeble, flickering light from a solitary electric bulb, two elderly men sat hunched on a concrete bench.

"The dungeons!" hissed Flame-Red.

Through the next window, the scene was the same. At the third window, the only difference was the presence of a young boy with an older man. And so it went on, window after window, dungeon after dungeon. And always, the inhabitants were either elderly or young.

As Toby and Flame-Red hovered by the tenth window, Flame-Red drew in a sharp breath. "Tally!"

A little boy with curls as orange as Flame-Red's glanced up. The other occupant, an elderly man, rose to his feet and hobbled towards the window. He squinted through the bars with small eyes set in a heavily lined face. Long white hair fell down his back, and his beard touched his knees.

"Wizard Greystone!" Flame-Red jabbed the air with her finger, bursting their bubble.

What was she doing? It wasn't safe to be visible. Toby gave her a sharp pinch, but she ignored him.

The man flinched at their abrupt appearance.

"Flame!" cried the little boy, rushing to the window.

"Shhh, Tally," said Flame-Red. "We don't want anyone to hear."

He reached upwards through the bars, and Flame-Red stretched down, but their hands didn't meet.

"I've got Marvin," said Flame-Red. "Not here. In a field nearby. He misses you."

Tears swam in the boy's eyes.

"We'll get you out soon," she said. "Don't you

111

worry."

The man cleared his throat. "You found us then?" He gestured towards Toby. "Who is this?"

"This is Toby, the boy who rescued Witch Skylark," said Flame-Red. "Toby, this is Wizard Greystone, our Head Wizard."

"My dear boy!" said the wizard. "We remain eternally grateful for your help."

Toby gave a small, embarrassed smile. However, inside, a spark of pride surged through him. This was certainly better than the mistrustful reaction of the witches in Little Witchery.

"And is your mother here?" Wizard Greystone turned his attention back to Flame-Red.

Her shoulders drooped. "Captured."

"And the others?"

"Three captured. The rest are in Little Witchery."

"And you don't have a warbler, so you are stranded here?" said the Head Wizard.

Flame-Red nodded.

He rubbed his beard. "Well, this is a fine mess indeed."

Toby leant down to the window. "Why have they brought you here? What are they doing?"

"I am yet to work that out," said Greystone slowly. "But, do you know, I don't think the whole wyzine clan is here." He glanced towards the cell door. "On the rare occasions we're let out for fresh air, only the elderly and young are amongst us. I haven't seen your father at all, Flame-Red."

She opened her mouth to reply when the wizard cocked his head, listening.

Voices sounded in the corridor. "And you've had interest in the witches?" said one.

"From a royal family no less. If we play our cards right, the Head Witch and the bumbling one will be off to Denmark in a few days," replied another.

Wizard Greystone flapped at the window. "You have to go!"

Before Toby had time to grasp Flame-Red's waist, the hovering broom revved into action. As it soared upwards, he slipped straight off the end. His foot struck the window bars, and a metal arm shot out of the grassy wall, grabbing his ankle.

Noooo! He mustn't be caught. Toby wriggled and thrashed, but the claw around his leg held firm.

He dangled upside down, the blood draining to his head.

He was trapped.

CHAPTER EIGHTEEN

An ear-splitting alarm rang in the SMI.

Shouts echoed inside. "Intruder! Intruder!"

Wizard Greystone reached through the bars, desperately trying to release the claw, but it wouldn't budge.

Flame-Red and the broom circled and dropped again. She couldn't free Toby either.

The claw was tightening around his ankle, piercing his skin.

The alarm wailed louder.

"Hold still!" Flame-Red took a potion from her pouch and, hands shaking, splashed several drips onto the metal arm.

With a sizzle, the arm melted away. Toby collapsed onto the back of the broom just as Mr Dackman and another man strode round the side of the hill.

Flame-Red waved her wand, and in an instant, she and Toby were invisible. The broom took off with the claw still attached to his ankle, like some alien body part. It weighed a tonne and they couldn't get more than a couple of metres off the ground. With every bump of the broom, the pincers dug deeper until he was whimpering in pain.

Flame-Red landed a little way up the road, and he slithered off.

"Your leg!" she said.

Blood was trickling onto his foot.

Teeth gritted, Flame-Red pulled and twisted, but the claw wouldn't budge.

The two men appeared at the end of the road. Mr Dackman held an object in the air, and it beeped.

A small red light lit up on the claw.

"This way," said Dacker's dad.

A shudder ran down Toby's spine. "They're tracking it!"

He tried to drag himself away, but the metal was too heavy, his ankle too painful.

Flame-Red was desperately searching through her potions. "I can't melt it – it might melt your skin too." The vials clinked together. "What else can I use? What else?"

The men came closer.

"You'll have to leave me!" said Toby.

"No!"

"It'll be much worse for you if you're captured."

Mr Dackman pressed a button on the tracker, and the claw beeped again.

As the red light flashed, Toby had an idea. "My water bottle," he mumbled through the pain.

Flame-Red dug it out of his bag, and he poured it over the claw. The light flickered before dying altogether.

Dacker's dad stopped walking. "The signal's gone." He waved the tracker around.

"Let's continue in the same direction," said the other

115

man.

Toby and Flame-Red exchanged fearful glances. Ten more metres and the men would be upon them and burst their invisibility cover.

A flutter of black wings flitted above their heads.

The tracker in Mr Dackman's hand beeped.

"It's that blasted bat again!" he said. "It's interfering with the signal. I really thought it was an intruder this time. Wait until I get my shotgun out." He mimed shooting into the sky.

With a sigh, the two men turned on their heels and strode back towards the SMI.

"Barnaby's squeaks must be the same frequency as the tracker!" said Toby. A wave of dizziness swept over him, and he flopped onto the verge.

"We need to get this thing off you." Flame-Red tugged again at the claw.

"Penknife," he muttered. "Backpack pocket."

She passed it to him, and he poked the blade into the mechanism. His ankle throbbed as he prodded and fiddled, working himself free. Finally, with a click, the claw sprang apart.

Blood was still dribbling down his leg. What could he use as a bandage? He rummaged through his pockets: a dirty tissue. Nope. Try again. A purple piece of material. The patch from Bumble's dress which had held Willow's ring. Perfect. Toby wrapped it tightly round his ankle.

He sat, his breathing slowly returning to normal.

Flame-Red was already on her feet, bouncing around like a firecracker about to go off. "Where's my father if he's not in the dungeons? And what's Denmark? Why are they taking my mum there?"

"It's another country. And I have no idea! I heard the same as you," said Toby.

Flame-Red tore at her hair till it looked even more wild than normal. "We can't let it happen! We have to get her out." She paused, and her eyes flashed. "If you're going to help, that is. Otherwise, I'll do it myself."

Toby rubbed his forehead. This was all a massive mess, and once again, he was trapped at the centre of it. The SMI didn't seem to be experimenting on the wizards, but what *were* they doing? Why weren't all the wizards there? And now Willow and Bumble were going to be taken to another country?

Willow. Bumble. His friends.

They'd helped him so much over the past year. Because of them, he'd been able to rejoin his football team, spend time with Roger and Jazz, live a little. There was no way he could leave them to the clutches of the SMI. Hadn't he known that deep inside, ever since they'd been captured yesterday? And how could he abandon Flame-Red now? She could have left him with the claw round his ankle, but she hadn't.

"I'm in," he said.

"You're in what?" said Flame-Red.

"It means I'll help."

She gave a nod. "Thank you … Did you see how scared Tally looked?" The words caught in her throat. "He's my brother. I can't bear to think of him locked in a dungeon."

Toby stood up, testing the weight on his ankle. He picked up the broom. "The sooner we rescue them, the better. But first of all, we need to work out where the rest of the wizards are and exactly what the SMI is up to."

At the lake, Toby tumbled onto the grass, unable to put any weight on his ankle.

Still tied to the tree, Gemeralda glared at them. She tried to shift her position, and a grunt escaped her.

"She needs to stretch her legs," said Toby.

Flame-Red folded her arms. "She'll be fine."

"I know your mums are opponents. I know you don't trust her. But we can't treat her like this."

"All right. All right. I'll walk her round the lake," Flame-Red said with an exaggerated sigh.

She waggled her pouch of potions at Gemeralda as she untied her. "One false move, and I'll transform you to the size of an ant." They set off, Flame-Red with the tip of her wand pointed at Gemeralda's back.

Toby leant against the tree, trying to ignore the pain in his ankle. As he straightened out his leg, something dug into him: A small sack, half hidden in the long grass. Gemeralda's? He started to open it before stopping. He shouldn't. Then again – maybe it would explain what she was up to.

Marvin yawned and trotted over to sniff the bag. That settled it; if Marvin thought it was of interest, Toby would have to investigate.

He peered inside. Food! And quite a bit of it. Why had Gemeralda needed to take it on holiday to Wildhaven? Didn't the wizards feed them enough? There was a whole bunch of tibtabs, so plump they were bursting. Toby's mouth watered.

Beneath the food, he found another flare and some more rope. She'd come so prepared. Why? Ebonia had had a whispered conversation with Gemeralda before they'd left Little Witchery – what had she said? Something about a plan. *Think, think.* But the rest refused to come to him.

As Toby retied the sack, something rattled. He reopened it and dug around.

Empty.

His fingers caught on a rough edge in the lining – a hidden zip! Inside sat a small metal dial with a rotating arrow. A compass. But not a normal compass: at the top, instead of 'North', the arrow pointed to 'SMI'.

When the two witches returned, Toby held out the compass. "Why do you have this?"

"Why did you go through my sack?" Gemeralda's eyes blazed.

Flame-Red studied the object. "What does it do?"

"It shows the direction to the SMI," said Toby. "Whichever way you're facing, the arrow points to it."

Flame-Red drew in a sharp breath. "She has something to direct her to the SMI?"

"I found it," said Gemeralda. "When I was following you at the start. In the lane outside the SMI."

Flame-Red turned the compass over. On the back, a message had been inscribed in spidery handwriting: '*You know where to find me*'.

"That's witches' handwriting!" exclaimed Flame-Red.

Toby chewed his lip. "Earthens sometimes write like that too."

"I told you. I found it," said Gemeralda.

Flame-Red grabbed the rope. "I'm keeping a close eye on you."

She was about to wind it back round Gemeralda and

the tree when Toby held out a hand. "Wait. We can't keep Gemeralda tied to the tree forever. Maybe we can lock her in the cabin with the key Marvin found."

Flame-Red shook the rope at him. "She was going to tie *us* up."

Toby could almost see the steam coming out of Flame-Red's ears. "Doesn't mean you have to be as bad."

"Do you always have to be so reasonable?"

"Look what the rope has done to her wrists."

Flame-Red gave Gemeralda a push. "In the cabin! Now."

Gemeralda stomped into the cabin, brushing away the low-hanging ivy.

With a loud clunk, Flame-Red pushed the wooden door shut and turned the key.

CHAPTER NINETEEN

Toby stood on the country lane between Brocklehurst village and the SMI. He rubbed his back after another night spent sleeping on the ground. Who would have thought he'd long for his mattress with all the springs poking out? He'd even missed the bouncy moss floor of the cabin, but at least Gemeralda had a bit of space to move around now.

For the umpteenth time, Toby strained to see down the road. He'd been waiting on this grassy verge for nearly two hours now. Maybe the postman wasn't going to come? Perhaps the SMI didn't receive letters. In which case, this plan – Toby's one and only idea to find out more information – would be useless.

Flame-Red was a little further along the lane in her invisible bubble. He'd given her instructions of what a postman would look like – red clothes, maybe a red trolley or van. Surely she couldn't get it wrong?

A car approached, and Toby crouched down, pretending to tie his shoelace. His ankle gave a sharp twinge. The wound had scabbed over, but it was still tender and bruised. The car passed, and Toby straightened up. He pulled his baseball cap firmly onto his head to cover his hair. Nothing like having a blond mohican to make yourself easily recognisable. *Thanks, Bumble.*

"Well, well, well. If it isn't Bean!" said a voice behind him.

Toby flinched. He knew that voice. There was only one person who said his surname like that. But that person didn't belong in Oxfordshire.

He turned to see a familiar, fair-haired boy smirking at him. "What are *you* doing here, Bean?"

Really? It was the school holidays, Toby was far from home, and he still couldn't escape Darren Dackman?

"What are *you* doing here?" replied Toby. As soon as the words left his mouth, he knew the answer. Dacker must be helping his dad with the SMI. But that meant Dacker knew about the wizards? Knew about magic?

Dacker shrugged. "I'm on holiday."

"Me too," said Toby.

"Who with? You don't have any family … apart from your mum, and she can hardly travel, can she?" sneered Dacker.

"Just some friends," muttered Toby.

"I'm with my *father*. He's got important business."

Toby's jaw tightened. Had Dacker emphasised the word 'father' solely to rub Toby's nose in it?

"I tried out for Radton Rangers last week," said Dacker.

What? Radton Rangers was Toby's football club. His chance to run like the wind, be free of everything – including school bullies, like this one.

"They said I'm the fastest person they've ever seen. They think I'll make a great striker. Though they might

122

have to replace their current one." A smug smile played on Dacker's lips.

Toby's stomach lurched. *He* was Radton's striker. And he was *way* faster than Dacker. Surely this couldn't be right. Dacker must be trying to wind him up.

"Want me to prove it?" said Dacker. "I'll race you."

Toby turned away. He would *not* let Darren Dackman get to him. Ignoring him was the best policy.

Toby's backpack was wrenched so hard from his shoulder, he stumbled over. And there was Dacker sprinting down the road with his bag.

There was only one thing Toby could do. He gave chase.

He dashed after Dacker, his shoes pounding on the verge. Every step sent a jolt of pain through his ankle. But something else was wrong too. He should be able to catch Dacker – even with the leg injury. But the boy was galloping along in a whole different gear. It was like he'd gained superspeed.

Toby dug deep, put on an extra spurt, but still couldn't keep up.

Dacker ground to a halt, not even panting, and threw Toby's backpack onto the lane. "See you at trials, Bean," he said and stalked off.

Toby doubled over, clutching his side. *What had just happened*? Dacker, faster than him? This didn't make sense. Was he going to take his position on the team? Toby limped back up the road, dark clouds circling above.

As he reached his earlier position, someone hissed in his ear, and he jumped so vigorously, he bit his tongue.

A giggle came from beside him.

"Don't do that!" he said.

"Sorry," said an invisible Flame-Red. "But I think the postman's coming. Quick!"

Toby sprang to attention and strolled along the verge. A few seconds later, bicycle wheels whirred behind him. As the postman passed, Toby called: "If you've got anything for the SMI, I'm going that way."

The postman skidded to a halt. "Y'alright, mate. Wish I could say yes; I'm running late – blimming van broke down. But it's against postie rules and all that."

"Looks like you've got a lot of parcels there," said Toby. "They'll take you ages."

"It's that dratted woman in Olive Lane. Thinks I'm her personal delivery service." The man checked his watch and sighed. "You said you're heading past the SMI?"

"Yep."

The man delved into his bag. "Just this once. Don't tell on me, hey? You'll save me a trek." He withdrew a pile of letters, examined the addresses and handed a few to Toby. Then he leaned in. "What does it do, the SMI? Appeared a few months ago, hidden all the way out here."

"Sorry," said Toby. "I've no idea."

"Can't be locals. No one from Brocklehurst would build a hill over those caves; they're unstable. Oh well, I guess I'll discover more at some point. Maybe they're hiding aliens!" The man chuckled to himself.

Toby shook his head. If only he knew.

The postman put his feet back on the pedals. "Right, best be off, else I'll be even later. Make sure you deliver those letters straightaway." He cycled away, his legs pumping vigorously.

There was a popping sound, and Flame-Red

materialised by Toby's side. "You got them! Witchtastic. Let's read them."

She clambered over the stone wall opposite.

Toby hesitated. Was he going to get the postman into trouble?

"Come on," hissed Flame-Red.

He followed her, and they leant against the wall.

Toby studied the envelopes: There were four. On one, the address was typed. On the other three, it was handwritten. *Weird.* Who wrote business letters by hand these days?

Flame-Red leaned over his shoulder. "Go on then! Open them."

Toby's fingers hovered over the typed envelope. Was stealing someone else's letters illegal? Would he be put in prison if he was caught? Mum needed him at home.

Flame-Red grabbed it and tore it open.

"Wait!" cried Toby. "I was going to post them back to the SMI once we'd finished."

She dropped the ripped envelope into a cowpat.

So much for that plan.

Flame-Red held out several sheets of printed paper and frowned. "What is it?"

Toby scanned the first page: Rows of numbers in columns called payments and deposits.

"It looks like a bank statement," he said.

"A what?" said Flame-Red.

"People keep their money in a bank account. This shows everything that was paid into and out of the account in the past month."

Toby flicked through the rest of the pages, and his mouth dropped open.

"What? What's wrong?" asked Flame-Red.

"According to this, in the past month, the SMI have received…" he paused while he counted, "…one hundred payments of five thousand pounds. One hundred payments! Of five thousand pounds! That's half a million quid."

"Is that a lot?"

"It's a massive amount! I could buy Mum a nicer house. One with a balcony off the bedroom and a view of the countryside. I could buy all the food we need. I could…" Toby's mind wandered. *Half a million pounds.* He could buy football boots that didn't leak. He could pay for somebody to come and help while he was at school. And he'd still have enough to fill a pool full of banknotes and dive into it. He gave a wry smile.

When he glanced up, Flame-Red was watching him with a sympathetic look.

Toby pressed his lips together. He did not need her pity. He buried his head back in the bank statement.

"So why are they receiving so much money?" she asked.

"I'm not sure. It doesn't say who the payments are from."

The witch picked up the second envelope, and before Toby could say, "Careful", she'd ripped it open.

He sighed. Though, to be honest, stealing post was the least of his worries. If they planned on breaking the wizards out, he could be going to prison for a whole lot longer.

Flame-Red unfolded the letter and read aloud:

Dear Sir,

I write to accept your invitation to the Brocklehurst Hotel on the eighth of August at seven p.m. I will be attending along with my wizard aide.

Yours,
The Duke of Southampton.

"Wizard aide?" Flame-Red furrowed her brow. "What does that mean?"

Toby shrugged and reread the letter. "The Brocklehurst Hotel. I think we passed that in the centre of the village the day we arrived. I wonder what's happening there on the eighth. When is that, anyway? We left Little Witchery on the fourth..." He counted on his fingers. "Which makes it the eighth tomorrow!"

He put the letter aside and reached for the next one, but Flame-Red beat him to it. She pulled out another handwritten note in swirly script:

Dear SMI,

I write on behalf of the Prime Minister...

"The Prime Minister!" exclaimed Toby, leaning in to get a closer look.

"Who's that?"

"He runs the whole country. Like your Head Witch, I guess."

I write on behalf of the Prime Minister with regard

to your invitation for the eighth of August. Rest assured
that he will endeavour to attend, provided his schedule
allows. I am instructed to inform you that he is delighted
with his new employee and sends his utmost thanks.

Yours sincerely,
Secretary to the Prime Minister

Wizard aide. Employee. The realisation of what was
going on at the SMI hit Toby like a bombshell, and cold
dread trickled through him.

"Employee?" said Flame-Red.

"I think…" began Toby. "I think the SMI is hiring
out some of the wizards to work for important people."
He rifled through the bank statement again. "I bet that's
what all these payments are – the SMI gets paid five
thousand pounds each month per wizard."

"How can they do that!" cried the witch. "The
wizards don't belong to them. They're not their servants."

Nausea settled in the pit of Toby's stomach. Flame-
Red was right – how could the SMI do this? The wizards
were people, just like Earthens. They weren't some
commodity to be bought and sold. And there was worse.
It wasn't only the SMI who was doing this. The military
and the government were in on it too.

Toby's train of thought was broken by voices on the
road. Flame-Red's startled eyes met his own. They'd
been so preoccupied by the letters they hadn't paid
attention to what was going on around them. There was
no time for an invisible bubble. They dived onto their
tummies and pressed themselves into the wall.

CHAPTER TWENTY

"Denmark has paid the first instalment," said a female voice.

"Excellent, excellent."

Toby flinched. That second voice sounded like the Director.

"They're expecting the two witches on the ninth."

Next to Toby, Flame-Red's whole body stiffened.

"America is interested too. They've put in a request for several, for high-ranking officials," said the woman.

The Director gave a wry laugh. "At this rate, we'll need to capture the rest of the witches sooner rather than later."

"I'm working on it, JB," said the woman.

Their words and footsteps faded as they walked past and out of earshot. As soon as it was safe, Flame-Red jumped up and squinted down the road, but the figures had disappeared around a bend. "I'm sure I recognise the woman's voice," she said, peering vainly into the distance.

"How could you?" said Toby. "You don't know any Earthens."

Flame-Red frowned. "I don't know, but it sounds familiar."

Suddenly she let out a roar and kicked a stray stone high in the sky. It flew up and up and then plummeted, almost hitting Toby on the head.

"Watch it!" he said.

"The ninth! My mum and Bumble are being taken away on the ninth. We have to do something before then." Flame-Red booted another stone, and it sailed halfway down the field.

"You should be on my football team."

"Football?"

"It's a game … with a ball…"

"My mum's going to become a servant, and you're thinking about games?"

There wasn't really a time when Toby *wasn't* thinking about football. Well, maybe not thinking about it, but it was always there, part of his bones, his muscle and flesh. Hopefully, Dacker's new running speed wouldn't spoil things – football provided a good distraction from Mum's health, and apparently from the fate of Willow and Bumble, too, now.

Toby gave himself a shake. He no longer hid from life. He needed to face it, like Flame-Red did. He opened the fourth and final letter. "I still don't understand why they're all handwritten. People type business letters. Why have they even replied by post? Everyone emails."

"Email?" said Flame-Red.

"On the internet."

"The whatnet?"

Toby sighed. "Doesn't matter."

He held the letter aloft, and they read it together:

Dear SMI Director,

Thank you for your invitation for the eighth of August. I am delighted to accept. I remain extremely grateful for the use of Wizard Tallbridge…

Flame-Red gasped.

"What? What is it?" said Toby.

She took a deep breath. "Wizard… Wizard Tallbridge is my father." She looked like she was desperately trying not to cry.

At least she had a dad, even if he was a servant. The thought entered Toby's head before he could stop it. He bit his lip. That wasn't the right attitude! Flame-Red's whole family was in danger.

Toby reached over to comfort her, then faltered. If Mum was upset, he would gently put his hand on hers. If it was Roger, he'd give him a couple of encouraging thumps on the back. But this was Flame-Red, a witch he barely knew. He went to pat her on the shoulder, abruptly changed his mind and pretended to scratch his neck instead.

Flame-Red gave a noisy sniff. "Let's read the rest."

I remain extremely grateful for the use of Wizard Tallbridge. He is proving to be an extremely valuable member of staff. As requested, I'm keeping his identity a secret. And I will continue to correspond only by post.

I look forward to the evening at the Brocklehurst

Hotel.

With warmest regards,
Lord Montgomery.

"That explains why they're not emailing," said Toby. "Looks like it's all hush-hush."

Flame-Red continued to stare at the piece of paper, reading the words over and over. "I don't get it. My father wouldn't stand for it. He's wandtastic with magic. He'd turn Lord Montgomery into a mouse in an instant."

So not only did she have a dad, but he was also apparently amazing? *Not that wandtastic if he got captured, though.* Toby stopped himself before he could utter the thought aloud. Instead, he said, "I guess their wands were taken off them."

"My dad would still break free."

"Maybe he's trapped in a dungeon, like the others."

"Then how would he be a servant for them?" Flame-Red glowered at the ground, and Toby half expected the grass to smoulder and burst into flames. Not that the witches could do that, but even after a year, they surprised him with new powers. He edged out of arm's reach, just in case.

Flame-Red was right, though. It didn't make sense. How were Lord Montgomery and the others – the Duke, the Prime Minister – making the wizards work for them? And there was another thing: why were people paying so much for wizards who, without a wand, could do no more work than anyone else?

Toby rubbed his forehead. They had so many unanswered questions. They could spy on the event at the

Brocklehurst Hotel tomorrow. That might bring more clues. But that gave hardly any time before Bumble and Willow were shipped off. Plus, it was another day and a half away, and Toby and Flame-Red were almost out of biscuits and raspberries. They couldn't survive solely on magical food. They'd have to break into Gemeralda's secret stash.

It had started to drizzle again. Flame-Red was on her feet now, prowling up and down. In the rain, her orange curls looked even more wild and mane-like. She stopped suddenly. "I want to go and see my dad."

"You don't know where he is," said Toby. "The letter is just signed Lord Montgomery."

Flame-Red brandished the piece of paper. "There's an address in the top corner. It says he's in Oxfordshire too."

Toby examined the address and, for the second time that week, wished his phone could connect to the Internet. Wait – he'd taken a photo of a map when they'd been in Oxford. The memory of Bumble and Barnaby causing absolute chaos in the town centre played out in Toby's mind and he couldn't help but smile. But now Bumble was wallowing in some damp, dark dungeon. And in two days, she was going to become a servant to the Danish royal family.

He grabbed his phone, opened the photo of the map and scanned through it. There was Oxford, and there was Brocklehurst. Toby scrolled through villages and villages, but none of them matched the address. He started again, zooming into the photo, taking it centimetre by centimetre, until – "Here it is!" He showed Flame-Red his screen. "Montgomery Hall is actually marked on the map.

It must be enormous. Can you get us there?"

Flame-Red studied the map and then surveyed the landscape around them. "If Brocklehurst is in that direction…" she muttered, "that means we're here … so if we fly over this hill, follow the stream, pass over those houses… Right! Got it. Let's go."

She picked up her broom and climbed aboard. And for the first time, when Toby took hold of her waist, she didn't even flinch.

CHAPTER TWENTY-ONE

It continued to drizzle as they flew towards Montgomery Hall. Raindrops bounced off their invisible bubble and trickled down the sides. The bubble made a brilliant umbrella, but it was becoming smeared with water. Windscreen wipers would have come in handy right now. Flame-Red leaned forwards, squinting to see where they were going. They dropped height to avoid a flock of geese and nearly collided with an electricity pylon.

"Watch it!" cried Toby.

"You try steering in the rain!"

Steering wasn't the only problem, though – what if the raindrops on the bubble were making it visible? If anybody looked up, would they think a UFO was flying through the sky? And what if the rain became heavier – would that burst the bubble?

As they skimmed over a cluster of roofs, the drizzle reduced to a patter before stopping altogether. And there, through the blurry bubble, stood an enormous house on the horizon. No, not a house – a mansion, a palace, a castle. The closer they flew, the more magnificent it became. Grey stone walls rose to a flat roof, sided by battlements and a turret at each corner. A long driveway

135

twisted and turned through acres of parkland, sweeping up to an immense wooden door.

Toby gasped at the sight.

Montgomery Hall.

Flame-Red landed the broom in nearby trees, and they scrambled off, the bubble bursting as they did so. Toby gave his head a shake; being invisible always made him feel spaced out.

"Do all Earthens have houses like this?" asked the witch, her mouth wide.

Toby gave a bitter laugh. "Nope. You could fit a hundred of mine into it."

He counted the windows on the ground floor – fifteen, and that was just on this side. Plus, the building was three stories high. It felt like another world, almost as surreal as stepping into Little Witchery for the first time. How could this be one person's house? How could anyone have the money to own such a place?

"Ready to find my dad?" said Flame-Red.

"I guess so," said Toby.

She whispered the bubble spell, and they emerged from the safety of the trees. The grounds were quiet and deserted. The hall looked still and silent, though it was too far away to be sure. As they crept across the lawn, the hair on Toby's arms prickled. They were in the middle of a huge open space, the size of a football pitch. It felt so exposed, even though they were invisible. Every window in the building was an eye, piercing right through him.

They tiptoed closer and closer, but there were no signs of life, no noise but the twitter of birds. Imagine Mum waking up here each day rather than being surrounded by the busy streets outside their house.

The door loomed in front of them. It was decorated in intricate, carved patterns with two giant lion heads for knockers.

Flame-Red peered through a window to the left of it, and Toby joined her.

Black and white stone slabs lined the floor like a chessboard. They shone with polish and looked as treacherous as an ice-skating rink. Two tall vases stood either side of a double-width staircase which was covered in plush, purple carpet.

What an entrance hall. It was like stepping back in time.

Toby's imagination spun. He didn't normally get carried away – he left that to Roger – but he could practically see the gowned ladies gliding down the stairs. The gentlemen in tuxedos and tails waiting to escort them to dinner. And if Toby turned, there'd be a horse and carriage trotting up the driveway.

Flame-Red hissed his name, and he blinked and fell back to Earth.

She was beckoning him to the next window.

This room seemed to be a living room – what did posh people call them? Sitting room? No, drawing room, that was it. It was bigger than Toby's lounge and kitchen put together. In the middle of the room lay two sofas covered in red velvet with an arm at one end. There was a special name for them. Toby wracked his brains. Chair… chaise… chaise lounge? No. Chaise longue? Where had he plucked that word from? It wasn't like he'd ever seen one.

Between the chaise longues stood a coffee table laid with a china teapot and cups. An ornate tapestry showing a man on horseback hung on one wall. The only thing Toby had on his wall at home were football posters.

The following window looked onto the same room. The next two showed an enormous dining table with at least twenty seats. Large ancestral portraits in gold gilt frames hung from a picture rail.

All these rooms! All this space. And nobody using it.

Roger had to share his bedroom with his younger brother. Some people didn't even have that, sleeping on park benches or in shop doors. But this Lord Montgomery, he had enough space to accommodate most of England, and he had it all to himself.

There was one more room on this side of the building. It, too, was empty of human life, housing nothing but a grand piano.

Toby and Flame-Red rounded the corner of Montgomery Hall. It. Was. Vast. It stretched backwards almost as far as it did widthways.

Flame-Red peered through the first window and inhaled sharply.

"What?" Toby hurried to join her.

It was a small room – well, small compared to the ones they'd seen so far – with a bookshelf, a table and an armchair. And in the armchair sat a man with a moustache, gazing into space.

"My dad," gulped Flame-Red.

She rapped on the window, and her bubble burst.

Wizard Tallbridge's mouth fell open so wide Toby could have thrown a ball into it.

The wizard stumbled to his feet, rushed over and pulled up the sash. Before he could say anything, Flame-Red climbed through and fell into his arms.

A surge of jealousy swept over Toby, and his legs nearly gave way. What must it be like to hug your own dad? To feel safe in his hold? Toby gripped the wall to steady himself, and the rough bricks dug into his palms. The pain anchored him as waves undulated inside.

Flame-Red rested her orange curls against her dad's chest. Wizard Tallbridge didn't look anything like his daughter: he was tall and had fair hair. Toby stood up a little straighter – at least Mum said he and his dad had had the same brown hair. They'd even shared the same white tuft at the nape of their neck. But when Flame-Red drew back and her father regarded her with such love, Toby's body drooped again – what did it matter whether he looked like his dad if he wasn't even alive?

Wizard Tallbridge held Flame-Red by the shoulders and studied her face. "What's happened? Why are you here?"

"We arrived at the caves for our annual trip," she began.

Her father shot a nervous glance towards the study door, and Flame-Red lowered her voice. "Only you weren't there. We found an Earthen who had been turned into a mouse, and he directed us to Brocklehurst. So six of us set off. Well, seven actually, I suppose, though we didn't know about one of them. The rest of the clan returned to Little Witchery. At Brocklehurst, we found a building in a hill where some of the wizards are being kept captive."

"Are they all right?"

"They're underground, trapped in dungeons."

"And where is your mother?"

"Captured." Flame-Red's voice wobbled. "And in

139

two days, she's being sent to another country. To be a servant to the royal family."

"I see." Wizard Tallbridge's lips twitched, but he remained as composed and dignified as Witch Willow always did.

Toby shifted from one foot to the other. Flame-Red seemed to have forgotten he was even there.

"So, how did you find me?" asked Tallbridge.

"We intercepted the SMI's post; that's the place where the wizards are. And we found out you were here," said the witch.

"We?"

"Oh, I forgot! Toby's here too. He's the one who rescued Witch Skylark." Flame-Red pointed her wand towards the window and chanted:

Remove his bubble
Let him be seen
No hiding here
With invisible screen.

Toby's bubble burst with a pop. "Hey! It's not safe." He checked the grounds behind, but they were still deserted. He edged closer to the building, trying to blend into the wall.

"Toby, this is my dad. Dad, this is Toby." Flame-Red clutched the wizard's arm proudly.

The simmering jealousy inside Toby threatened to erupt. He wanted to throw something, to punch the wall. How could he feel such longing for something he'd never even had? He clenched his fists into tight balls.

"Pleased to meet you, Toby," said Wizard

Tallbridge.

Toby forced a smile.

Suddenly, footsteps sounded in the corridor, and they all jumped. Tallbridge pushed Flame-Red to the window. "Out! Out!"

She scrambled over the rim and threw a bubble round her and Toby just as the door to the room was flung open.

CHAPTER TWENTY-TWO

A portly man with a bald head and red cheeks strode inside. He wore tweed trousers and a waistcoat, the buttons gaping over his rotund belly.

Lord Montgomery?

Behind him followed another man holding a young woman in a black dress and white apron. Her hair was straggly, and her eyes dim.

"How's it going, old chap?" boomed the first man.

Wizard Tallbridge didn't reply.

The man's nostrils flared. "I expect to be acknowledged when I address you!"

Next to Toby, Flame-Red flinched.

"I'm fine," muttered Tallbridge.

"You're fine, what?" said the man.

"I'm fine, *Your Lordship.*"

Definitely Lord Montgomery, then.

"Good, good. That's the spirit." The man twirled his walking stick in his fingers. "Now, I'm in need of a top-up."

"It's too soon." Tallbridge gestured to the woman. "She's not regained her strength since last time."

"She can have a longer break afterwards. I have an

important poker match this afternoon. Significant bets have been placed, and I need to win."

Tallbridge stood his ground. "If you keep draining this Earthen, she will go past the point of recovery."

"Just today. Be a good sport." Lord Montgomery wielded his stick menacingly. "Do I need to remind you what will happen if you don't comply?"

The second man dragged the woman into the centre of the room. Anguish filled Wizard Tallbridge's eyes.

"Oh, Dad, no," whispered Flame-Red.

"What's going on?" said Toby.

She shook her head.

Montgomery pulled a wand from his pocket and passed it to Tallbridge. "Go on."

The wizard approached the woman. "I'm so sorry," he said.

She tried to struggle, but the man was gripping her shoulders, and there was little fight in her.

Flame-Red's dad held his wand to her forehead, and her body sagged. His face grim, he murmured a spell:

Suck out her strength
Give us our fill
So we enhance
Our own life skill.

As he chanted, wisps of golden light seeped from the woman's mouth and nostrils. They drifted in the air, merging to form a shimmering cloud. Her arms fell limp to her sides, and her legs buckled. Tallbridge removed his wand, and the man let go. She crumpled onto the floor like a rag doll.

143

Toby thought he might throw up. *What had they done?*

Beside him, Flame-Red was breathing louder and louder, her chest expanding and her cheeks flushed.

Wizard Tallbridge placed his wand in the centre of the pulsing mist and spun it till it wrapped around the wand like candyfloss. He stepped towards Lord Montgomery and blew it into his face.

Montgomery inhaled deeply, and the golden cloud streamed into his mouth.

Flame-Red trembled with anger. She looked like she was about to explode. Any second now, she was going to break their cover. Toby grabbed her arm. He really needed to rugby tackle her to stop her doing anything stupid, but it would cause too much commotion.

"It tingles!" said the Lord with glee. "Every cell in my brain is quivering." He threw a hand over his eyes as if it was unbearable, then blinked several times. He studied the room, and a smile spread across his lips. "I can see every single hair in your moustache!" he said to Tallbridge. "I can see every fibre of the armchair, every water particle in that vase."

Flame-Red's dad ignored him and bent down by the woman, placing a cushion under her head.

Lord Montgomery pulled a pack of cards from his waistcoat pocket and threw it to the other man. "Quick! Try me."

The man held up one of the cards with its back to Montgomery.

He scrutinised it. "Eight of spades!"

Another card.

"Jack of hearts!"

144

Another one.

"Four of clubs!" Montgomery chuckled. "They won't know what's hit them at this poker match." He turned for the door before pausing. "Your wand, Tallbridge."

The wizard passed it to him without leaving the woman's side.

"Come, Geoffrey. Take her to her room." Montgomery made for the door, his walking stick tapping on the floorboards.

The man followed, carrying the woman in his arms.

Tallbridge sank into the chair and buried his head in his hands.

Flame-Red scrambled through the window and ran over to him. "Dad! The Life Source spell? How could you?"

"I'm sorry you had to see that, Flame," he said into his palms.

Toby leant through the window. "What does the Life Source spell do exactly?"

"It uses one person's energy to benefit another," said Flame-Red. "Whoever inhales it will become extremely talented at something."

"Talented?"

"You saw with *that* man. It improved his eyesight so much he could see through cards."

"You never know which skill it will enhance till you take it," said Tallbridge, looking up. "It could make you run as fast as the wind or hear as well as a fluttermouse."

Run as fast as the wind... An image of Dacker sprinting at an impossible pace down the road flew into Toby's mind. Then his thoughts went to the strange man who had been on the Dackmans' drive – a wizard? Had Dacker gained his speed through the Life Source spell?

"But it only enhances someone's skill at the expense of someone else," growled Flame-Red.

"The woman – what did it do to her?" asked Toby.

"It made her very weak, very poorly."

Weak. Poorly. Toby felt like his own life was being sucked out. It was bad enough people feeling unwell because of a biological illness like his mum. But now Earthens were inflicting it on others on purpose with magic? Just so they could become super talented at something? "The woman will get better – right?"

"She'll gradually recover over a few days, yes," said Tallbridge. "But not if Lord Montgomery keeps demanding more. Doing the Life Source spell too frequently means the victim will eventually become a shadow of their former self."

Toby wobbled. The woman was going to be ill forever. Just like Mum.

"And it's not only this woman," said Tallbridge. "Every household who has a wizard is using them for the same reason."

Toby leant heavily against the windowsill.

Hundreds of Life Source spells. Hundreds of people drained of energy.

"Why did you do it?" he asked Tallbridge.

"I didn't have any choice."

"He gave you your wand," said Flame-Red. "You could overpower him in an instant."

"You've seen they've imprisoned some of the wyzine clan? The old and the young?" said her father.

Toby and Flame-Red nodded.

"Well, the rest of us are servants," Tallbridge spat out the word. "And if we refuse to help or try and escape or use our magic against an Earthen, then…" He paused as if pondering his words. "Then something would happen to the wizards who are locked up."

"Something would happen?" asked Flame-Red frowning. "Like what?"

"Did you see Wizard Shield when you arrived at Wildhaven?"

Toby's insides did a flip. Wizard Shield had been shot, killed by the army.

"You don't mean… They wouldn't kill the wizards in the dungeons! Would they?" Flame-Red's last words were barely a squeak.

"It's what we've been told," said Tallbridge. "And I don't see why they wouldn't. They've done it before."

"But Tally is there!"

"I know, Flame, I know."

Flame-Red rubbed her eyes roughly. "We HAVE to get them out. Then you'd be free to escape too."

Toby straightened up. She was right. But it wasn't just about rescuing the wizards anymore. It was about saving hundreds of Earthens from the Life Source spell too … saving them from becoming like Mum. They had to stop the SMI. But how?

147

CHAPTER TWENTY-THREE

Tallbridge stood up. "There's nothing either of you can do. It's too dangerous. Flame-Red – you will return to Little Witchery."

"I'm not leaving!" she cried.

"Shh!" The wizard shot a worried glance towards the library door.

"Besides," Flame-Red lowered her voice, "I don't have a warbler, so I have no idea where Little Witchery is."

A lightbulb flicked on in Toby's brain. "What about Witch Hazel?"

"What about her?" said Flame-Red.

"Doesn't she have a warbler? She's staying with my mum. We can use hers to go back to Little Witchery and get help to rescue the wizards."

"She doesn't have one," said Flame-Red. "Can't get the hang of them."

No surprise there. Toby had seen Hazel's attempts at using simple kitchen gadgets. His spirits sank. It really was down to him and Flame-Red.

He racked his brains. "What's happening tomorrow evening? Something at the Brocklehurst Hotel?"

"Some sort of drinks party for all the employers and their *servants*," said Tallbridge in disgust. "An opportunity, no doubt, for them to show off. See whose wizard has given them the best talent."

Toby's mind whirred. "Does that mean everyone will be there? The SMI employees, the high-up people, the wizards who are working for them?"

"I believe so…" said Tallbridge.

A spark lit up in Flame-Red's eyes. "So all the awful Earthens involved in this will be in the same room at the same time?"

Toby nodded slowly – was she thinking what he was thinking?

"You're wondering what if something rather unfortunate might happen to them?" said Tallbridge.

"You could do a spell," said Flame-Red. "And if they're all together, there'll be no one to harm the rest of the wizards in the dungeons. Then you can all escape."

Tallbridge shook his head. "I won't have my wand. Lord High-and-Monty will have it. But *you* could perform a spell on them, Flame."

"I couldn't! I'm terrible at spells," she wailed.

The room descended into silence.

Toby's stomach rumbled. He clutched it, but it went on and on like one of Bumble's steam train snores.

"Have you two been surviving solely on magical food?" asked Tallbridge.

"Mostly, apart from some Earthen biscuits and rubyberries we found," said Flame-Red.

Toby opened his mouth to correct her before deciding better of it. It was best to pick your battles with the witches. Besides, rubyberries was a much better name

149

than raspberries, though he'd never tell her that.

Tallbridge strode over to a fruit bowl and plucked two bananas off a large bunch. "Have these. Lord Monty won't notice."

"I don't know what this is, but I'm too hungry to care," said Flame-Red, taking a massive bite into the skin.

"Wait!" said Toby. "You're supposed to…"

She spat out a mouthful of banana skin and mush with a "Slimy slugs!"

"…peel them," finished Toby.

He showed her how to do it, and she took a very tiny, very careful bite. She chewed it, rolling it around her tongue.

Toby devoured his whole banana in four giant mouthfuls. Not his favourite food, but it was fine. Right now, even a plate of nimnucket stew would taste good.

"Here, take a couple for later." Tallbridge passed them two more from the bowl.

"We better take one for Gemeralda, too," said Toby.

Flame-Red scowled. "I suppose."

"What?" said her dad. "You're not alone?"

"It's a long story."

"Try me," said Tallbridge before whipping around towards the library door. "Someone's coming."

The footsteps grew louder, passed the room, and faded into the distance.

"It's not safe for you to stay here," said Tallbridge.

"But we haven't worked out what we're going to do!" cried Flame-Red.

"You know, you don't seem that bad at spells," said Toby. "You do the bubble one fine. Maybe you *could* do something at the hotel event."

150

"I can do the bubble one because I've had thousands of times to practise it. I can't do a new spell on hundreds of people."

"How about a potion then?" said Toby.

Flame-Red darted a glance towards her dad.

"Potions? You've been working on potions?" said Tallbridge.

She wrung her hands. "I find them easier than spells. Mum doesn't know. All she cares for is spells. I'm not good enough for her."

"Flame," said her dad. "That's not true! She just wants the best for you. Potions can be perilous – you need a special knack to do them."

"Flame-Red's good at it," said Toby. "I've seen her use them."

She shot him a look which almost burnt through his chest and clutched the small bag in her pocket.

"You've brought some with you?" Annoyance flitted across Tallbridge's face.

Uh oh. Toby edged backwards. Flame-Red had asked him to keep that a secret.

"One hair too many, one millisecond of moonlight too long, and you could blow your eyebrows off. Why, you could blow your whole head off," said the wizard.

"I haven't yet, have I?" said Flame-Red grumpily.

Tallbridge rubbed a weary hand over his forehead. "I should have known you find spells difficult – I'm your father! It isn't right we don't live together. Tally and I really miss you."

"I miss you too, Dad."

The raging jealousy in Toby eased a bit. Flame-Red might have a dad, but she rarely got to see him. Her father

151

knew hardly anything about her life. Why didn't the witches and wizards didn't live together?

"So, you're good at concocting?" Tallbridge said to Flame-Red. He gave a wry smile. "I knew you'd be trouble. Talented but trouble."

"Should I use one at the hotel tomorrow?" she said.

"It'd be risky, very risky," her dad replied. "If it goes wrong, we're putting the lives of all the wizards in peril."

"We don't have another option," said the witch.

"What potion would you use?" asked Toby.

"Make them tiny? Turn them into mice?" said Flame-Red.

"Can't you do something a little less permanent?" He'd be going to jail for life at this rate if they were caught.

"Hmm, I have an idea." Tallbridge lifted his daughter's curls and whispered in her ear.

Toby leant through the window but could only catch snippets of sentences: "…grow by a river…", "…tall with green spikes…"

"If you want me to help, I need to know what potion you're going to use," he hissed.

"Potion recipes are highly guarded," said Tallbridge and went back to whispering in Flame-Red's ear.

Heat flushed through Toby. This wasn't fair! All he'd done to help them, and now they were keeping secrets from him? He turned and stalked down the lawn. A statue stood by a pond: a portly man with a bald head, waistcoat and walking stick. It was the spitting image of Lord Montgomery. Well, apart from the fact it was made of grey stone.

How much must you love yourself to want a massive

statue of your own face in your garden? Plus, how much money must you have to waste? Toby swung his leg and gave the bottom a hefty kick. His big toe throbbed with pain. *Wonderful*. Just what he needed, another injury.

"Oi! You," shouted a gruff voice behind him.

Toby whipped round.

A man in green overalls hovered twenty metres away. "What are you doing, you little tyke?" He dropped the handles of his wheelbarrow and took a step forwards.

Toby's heart did a double thump. The most sensible thing to do would have been to smile nicely and make up an excuse. Say he was lost or something. The worst thing to do would have been to run. Running meant you were guilty. But Toby didn't have time to think. In a split second of panic, he did the thing he was best at: he ran.

CHAPTER TWENTY-FOUR

Toby sprinted around the statue and pond and across the manicured lawn. Heavy footsteps pounded behind, but Toby was fast. Fear spurred him on, and he didn't even notice the throbbing in his toe. He allowed himself a quick glance over his shoulder: the man was some distance away, stumbling in his wellington boots, yet he didn't look like giving up.

Ahead grew a high hedge with a gap in it. Toby made directly for the opening. He darted through and almost ran face-first into another hedge. *Huh?* He took a left, running between the two hedges. They suddenly turned abruptly, forcing him to turn too. Right, left, left again. Where were they taking him? Toby skidded to a halt – a dead end, surrounded on all sides by thick hedges. He'd run straight into a maze. And he was trapped.

Somewhere behind him came the gardener's panting breath. Toby skittered backwards. *There must be another way out.* There, another opening in the hedge. He careered through it just as the man's green overalls turned the corner.

Left, right, straight on. Toby needed to get out of here, but he seemed to be heading deeper and deeper into the labyrinth. It became dim and murky, the grey sky blotting out any light from above. Arms stretched in front, Toby rushed round and round, spiralling towards the centre of the maze. And then his hands smacked into a wall of spiky branches. Another dead end.

Stomping footsteps came nearer, and panic rose in Toby's chest. He'd managed to herd himself expertly into a pen like a sheep. The gardener staggered round the corner and doubled over, wheezing. Toby braced himself. Could he dodge the man and make a run for it? Just like avoiding a football tackle. But the hedges closed in on either side, and there wasn't any room to get past.

The man straightened up and glanced this way and that. "Where are you, you little thief?"

Toby frowned. The gardener had looked straight at him, yet hadn't noticed him. What was going on? And then Toby saw it, the slight haze in the air surrounding him. He was in an invisible bubble.

There came a pattering noise from further in the maze.

"Aha!" cried the man, blundering off.

A few seconds later, Flame-Red materialised, hovering above Toby. "I threw some pebbles to distract him. Now get on!"

As Toby pulled himself up, their bubbles burst. The sound of the gardener's footsteps came closer again. There wasn't time to clamber fully aboard. Flame-Red took off, with Toby hanging over the broom, his arms dangling one side, his legs the other.

They sped through the sky. Toby still hadn't caught his breath from his sprint across the grounds, and now he was swinging like a pendulum. In the cool air, the layer of sweat on his skin turned into a clammy film, and he began to shiver uncontrollably. He was going to be sick. He was going to splatter the world below with remnants of half-digested banana.

"Stop!" he yelled before clamping his mouth together.

Flame-Red slowed their speed and landed the broom in an isolated field. Toby slithered off, stumbled a few steps and retched into a corner. He retched again and again. When his tummy was completely empty, he crawled to a stone wall and slumped against it.

"I'm sorry you're caught up in all of this," whispered Flame-Red. "Thanks for all your help."

Toby gave a weak nod. He must look a dreadful sight, and he probably smelt like a pair of old football boots. But he didn't care. He hadn't had a good night's sleep for days. His ankle ached. And now he'd thrown up some of the only proper food he'd eaten.

'*Come on holiday,*' Bumble had said. '*It'll be fun,*' she'd said.

Yeah right. He continued to quiver.

"You're cold!" said Flame-Red. "Here, have this." She untied her cloak and wrapped it around him.

Toby tried to resist, but she insisted, so he let her. It had been so long since someone had looked after him. Every day he cared for Mum. He cooked, washed her hair, plumped her cushions. If she needed something doing, he had to do it. Not that it was her fault. Not at all. But right now, it felt lovely to be looked after, to have somebody else take responsibility.

Flame-Red rummaged through Toby's bag and brought out his bottle which they'd filled at a spring earlier. "Have some water."

He obediently took a few sips, and it soothed his raw throat.

They sat in silence for a while, Toby huddled in Flame-Red's cloak. It smelt faintly of her, and it was actually rather comforting.

Slowly, his tummy stabilised, and his strength returned. "What potion are you going to use at the hotel?"

Flame-Red chewed her lip. "I'm not supposed to tell you about our different concoctions, but we're thinking of a sleeping one. Send them to the land of wink for a few hours and give the wizards a chance to escape."

Toby considered this. "Can you give them something to erase their memories too? Otherwise, they'll come looking for the wizards as soon as it wears off."

"I hadn't thought of that." Her face paled. "Mixing two potions is hard. And I've never done a memory one."

Suddenly, an ear-splitting clap reverberated around the valley.

Flame-Red's eyes widened in terror.

"It's just thunder," said Toby.

"Or Witch Zazzle," muttered Flame-Red.

"Gemeralda's grandmother? The one on a cloud?"

"Yes. She's a dangerous witch. She was banished thirty years ago, but they say she's getting more powerful again. Thunder and lightning were her speciality."

Now it was Toby's turn to be alarmed. *A dangerous witch who could create thunder and lightning?*

Ominous black clouds rolled across the sky.

"You said she caused an uprising?" asked Toby.

"Like Witch Ebonia, she believed the wyline and wyzine clans shouldn't hide away. She believed we

157

should use our magic to control Earthens. Quite a lot of the wizards supported her. They stormed the main hall in Little Witchery and almost brought down the Council. The place was destroyed."

Toby shuddered. "What happened?"

"She was defeated. But it was close. Without Zazzle, the wizards lost the motivation to attack Earthens. But the the wyline clan thought it was safer to live apart. That's why the wizards moved to Wildhaven."

So that was why they didn't live together! No wonder Bumble had kept that quiet. He could see why she hadn't wanted him to know about a possible Earthen attack.

A flash of lightning streaked above their heads, followed by another crash of thunder.

"Where did you say this cloud is again?" Toby's voice quavered.

"A long way away. Over the North Pole."

Drops of water started to fall.

Flame-Red held out her hand, and they settled on her palm. "Looks like it's normal thunder. Witch Zazzle doesn't create rain."

Toby was about to ask more when the heavens fully opened, and a torrent of water fell from the skies.

Flame-Red waved her wand and cast bubbles around them. The rain hammered the tops like the drumming of a wild rock star. The bubbles wobbled, their surfaces billowing. And then they burst. Flame-Red tried to rebuild them, but the downpour was too strong, and they burst again and again.

Hastily, Toby unwrapped Flame-Red's cloak from his shoulders and held it over his head. "Come here!"

The witch hesitated, then shuffled forwards and

huddled next to him. The rain was driving in the sides, and they had to squash together to try and keep dry. It wasn't long before the cloak was drenched, and water came dripping through.

"Can't you do something?" yelled Toby over the deafening tumult.

"Like what?" Flame-Red shouted back. "I'm no good at spells. And we can't make something from nothing. I've already told you that."

As Toby held up the sodden material, cold rain trickled into his sleeves and ran in rivulets down his cheeks.

"Oh, this is ridiculous!" exclaimed Flame-Red. "I don't know why you're still holding the cloak; it's not doing a bit of good."

She sprang to her feet and stepped into the pouring rain. In seconds, she was drenched, her wild curls glued to her face in dark strands. She threw her arms open to the sky.

She'd lost it. She'd gone well and truly bonkers.

"Come on!" she cried.

Toby shrank backwards.

"You're shaking again. You need to move." Flame-Red grabbed his arm and hauled him to his feet.

She jogged up and down on the spot.

Toby stared at her, his teeth chattering.

"You'll get the freezles." Flame-Red poked him in the ribs. "Move!"

As he attempted to dodge her finger, Toby slipped on the wet grass. He swayed, trying to regain his balance, his arms circling like windmill sails. Then he faceplanted into a ditch.

He sat up, spitting out mouthfuls of dirt, his whole front plastered in mud from head to toe.

A peal of laughter rang in the air. "I'm sorry! I'm sorry, but you should see yourself," hiccupped Flame-Red.

Toby wiped his eyes with his hands, but they were as dirty as the rest of him, and he smeared more mud onto his face. He lifted his head to the sky, and the rain washed his skin clean.

Flame-Red stood a few metres away, biting her lip in an obvious attempt to stifle her giggles. "Are y…you…all right?" She let out another guffaw.

This was the last straw. He'd been chased. He'd thrown up. And now he was soaking wet. Toby scooped up a fistful of mud and hurled it at her.

It hit Flame-Red in the face, and her eyes widened in shock.

Now it was his turn to laugh.

Flame-Red, however, was quick to retaliate. Toby ducked her first throw, but the second struck him in the chest. Soon, mud was flying in all directions. They were shouting and yelling, and Toby wasn't sure if he was laughing, crying or both.

"Enough! Enough," Flame-Red spluttered, leaning over to catch her breath.

Panting, Toby lowered his hand which held another mud pie ready to fire.

"I surrender!" she called. "Drop your weapon."

"You're sure? You're not going to blast me as soon as I put it down?"

"Witch's honour! I can barely see anyway."

Toby let the mud slither to the ground with a splat.

"You look like a swamp-squelcher," said Flame-Red.

"Well, you look like a bog monster," said Toby.

They exchanged a grin. Who would have thought the grumpy lion could be fun? Flame-Red was like an onion. She had all these barriers up, but once you peeled them back, the inside was surprising.

The rain was easing now.

Dirt dripped off their chins, their clothes were heavy and caked in mud, and their shoes squelched with every step.

Toby peered hopefully upwards at the clearing skies, but there wasn't a ray of sun in sight. "I don't suppose you can do a drying spell, can you?" Willow had used one on him before, and it had worked a treat.

A shadow fell across Flame-Red's face, and Toby instantly regretted his words. "No spells," she said flatly. Then she brightened. "I do have a potion, though. One I created myself."

"Your own potion? Are you sure it's safe?" said Toby. Wizard Tallbridge had said you could blow your head off if you weren't careful.

Flame-Red scowled. "Perfectly safe." She pulled a vial from the pouch in her pocket. Pulsing away inside was an orangey-red liquid. "Want to try it?" She uncorked the bottle and held it out.

Toby drew back.

Flame-Red shrugged and squeezed two drops onto her own arm. They spread up her sleeve, onto her shoulder and across her red jumper, drying as they went. They travelled through her cheeks and down her bedraggled strands of hair, which sprang into corkscrews

161

even more wild than before – if that were possible. The last things to dry were her trousers and boots.

She gave a contented smile and brushed the now-dried mud off her clothes. It disintegrated into a crumbly powder.

Toby pulled at his sodden clothes. His pants were clinging to his bottom, and he was wet in places he didn't know existed. He held out a hand.

"Oh, so you *do* want some now?" said Flame-Red. "I thought you didn't trust it?" She popped the cork back in the bottle.

Toby grimaced. He was going to have to beg. "I'm sorry. You were right. Please can I have some potion?"

"I didn't quite catch that?"

"I said I'm sorry. You were right."

"There you go. Music to my ears." Flame-Red gave a wink and poured a couple of drops onto Toby's sleeve. As it spread into his body, warmth tingled through him. It was like gooey hot chocolate heating his insides. Soon, he was completely dry. He ran a hand through his hair. The stupid mohican seemed to be sticking up even higher.

Flame-Red was watching him. "What's that white patch at the back of your head?" she said.

Toby gritted his teeth. He *hated* people asking him about it. It reminded him how obvious it was, how weird it was. Mum told him to be proud of it. So did Bumble. But it was hard to be different. At least Dacker and his gang no longer used it as target practice.

"It's just a bit of hair that doesn't have any pigment," he said. "My dad had one too."

"Your dad?" said Flame-Red. "You've never mentioned him."

162

"He's dead." Toby shoved his baseball cap onto his head. "Shall we get back to the cabin?"

Flame-Red picked up her broom, a steely look in her eyes. "Let's go."

Toby clambered on behind. How could she be so confident? They had a massive task ahead. And they had to succeed.

CHAPTER TWENTY-FIVE

Back at the lake, Gemeralda was still in the cabin. She regarded them coldly as Flame-Red unlocked the door. At least she wasn't wet – the hanging ivy made a helpful cover.

Toby peeled one of the bananas and handed it to her. She must be ravenous, but she refused to eat it till he'd moved away.

Marvin was asleep by the tree. He stood up, stretched and wound himself round Flame-Red's ankles. She lifted him, and he licked her face before jumping down and stalking towards Gemeralda. He sat watching her, eyes narrowed and ears pricked.

Toby pulled Flame-Red out of earshot. "We can't keep Gemeralda locked up much longer."

"We can't release her yet. Look at Marvin; he doesn't trust her one bit. We'll let her go after tomorrow night – if we manage to free the wizards."

That was a BIG if.

Flame-Red stalked over to the cabin, shut the door and turned the key.

"So, this sleeping potion," Toby said. "Have you thought if you can combine it with a memory one?"

Flame-Red picked her fingernails. "I don't know. I'd have to make them both from scratch."

"What potions have you brought with you?" asked Toby.

"I shouldn't really show you."

"I've already seen three of them!"

Flame-Red wavered before opening the pouch and laying seven vials on the moss. She pointed to them each in turn: "*Enlargio* – you've seen that work on my cloak, *Fixissimo* – mends broken things, *Meltisse* – dissolves metal, *Flame* – the drying one."

"You've named one after yourself?"

Flame-Red's face flushed. "Well, I created it. It warms as well as dries." Her shoulders drooped, and she started to clear the vials away.

Drat. She had no confidence in her spells, and now he'd mocked her about her potions too. "I'm sorry! I'm sorry. It worked really well. Please show me the rest."

She hesitated.

Toby pointed to the fifth one. "What's that?"

"*Reductify*. It makes things little."

"And those two?" They were smaller than the rest, no bigger than a fifty pence piece, and each contained a tiny silver coil inside clear liquid.

"*Alarmis*. I invented them, too," said Flame-Red. "They're connected. If you shake one vigorously for a minute, the other vibrates too."

Toby picked one up and was about to shake it when she shouted, "Don't!"

He flinched and the bottle shot from his hands. He reached for it, knocked it with the tips of his fingers, and flicked it further into the air. Flame-Red gave a strangled cry as the bottle sailed through the sky. Toby dived to the ground, did a barrel roll through the tall, wet grass and caught it with outstretched arms.

Phew. That wouldn't have been good, mocking one potion and destroying another.

Flame-Red rolled her eyes, but a smile crept along her lips.

Toby held out the potion sheepishly.

After a pause, she said, "You should keep it."

"Huh?"

"They're a way of communicating. If one of us is in trouble, we can alert the other one by shaking the bottle."

Toby raised an eyebrow. "You trust me with it after what just happened?"

"Not really." Flame-Red winked. "But you should have it in case."

Toby wrapped the vial in a tissue and placed it carefully in his jeans' pocket. "So you can't use any of these to help make the sleeping or memory potion?"

Flame-Red shook her head. "I'll have to collect the ingredients tonight."

"Can't it wait till tomorrow?"

"They have to be picked in the dark and mixed in a pond in moonlight."

Obviously. Sometimes, the witches' magic sounded like a lot of fairy-tale hocus-pocus.

They laid out the remains of their food: two bananas, a handful of raspberries and four biscuits.

That would do now for the three of them. They could have some magical food too. Tomorrow they'd eat the tibtabs and the rest of the things Gemeralda had brought. That still wasn't loads though. Their energy levels needed to be high for the Great Wizard Rescue.

An idea sprang into Toby's brain. "The Enlargio potion – could we use it on food too?"

He and Mum could use it to double their supplies when things were tight, which was always.

"You can't ingest it," said Flame-Red. "It's not safe."

A lump caught in Toby's throat, and he turned away. Having more food would have made life so much easier. He swallowed down the lump and took a biscuit. Might as well enjoy their 'feast' before it was all gone.

Later that evening, as dusk fell, Flame-Red reached for her cloak. Toby stretched his limbs and got to his feet.

She held up her hand. "I'm going by myself."

"Are you sure?"

"We can't let you know what goes into the potion."

This again! After all the magic he'd experienced, and they were still hiding things from him? He was too tired to argue, though. And to be honest, curling up in his sleeping bag sounded a whole lot better than tramping around the countryside.

Marvin was sniffing the undergrowth nearby.

"Coming?" Flame-Red called to him.

His snout shot up, his large ears pricked.

"Keep safe," said Toby.

"I'll be fine." She strode into the night with Marvin trotting at her heels, and they were soon swallowed by blackness.

Toby watched with admiration. How could she be so brave? He would hate it.

He stood by the tree as the small light from Flame-Red's wand bobbed along. Then it too disappeared from sight. His ankle twinged, and he gingerly felt it. It was swollen but healing. Bumble's bandage patch had done the trick.

"What potion is she making?" came a voice.

Toby looked around in the gloom. Had Gemeralda just spoken? She'd barely said anything the whole time.

"Over here."

Toby gingerly approached the cabin.

Gemeralda's face was pressed against a gap halfway up the stone wall. A ray of moonlight burst through the clouds and glittered in her startling emerald eyes. "What does she need a potion for?"

Toby chewed his lip. He had no idea what was going on in her mind. Best to keep quiet.

"I don't see why you're helping her," said Gemeralda.

"Don't you want the wizards to be rescued? Four witches have been captured too!"

"So that's what you're intending to do."

Drat. He should have kept his mouth shut.

"It's not fair of Flame-Red, making you get involved," Gemeralda continued. "It's not your problem. You already helped the clan enough last year. And look where that got you! I hear you lost your house."

Toby bristled. How did she know that? Had the witches all been talking about him behind his back?

Gemeralda took on a coaxing tone. "Why don't you let me out, and then I can fly you home."

"I thought witches couldn't fly without their wand?" he said. Flame-Red had taken it off her days ago.

168

"Well, unlock the door, and we can get it back. You could get into so much trouble here. Your mum needs you."

Anger flared through Toby. How dare Gemeralda mention his mum! She knew nothing about his situation. Nothing! She was right, though. He mustn't get into trouble. Mum couldn't manage without him.

"I can help rescue the wizards instead of you," said Gemeralda. "In a few hours, you could be home safe, sleeping in a proper bed."

Toby fiddled with the cuff of his jumper. That sounded good, really good. She had a point – rescuing the wizards wasn't his responsibility. An image of Bumble chained up in one of the dungeons crept into his mind, but he dispelled it. Gemeralda could help instead of him.

"Did you see the men had guns the other night?" she said. "You should get away from the danger."

The scene played out in Toby's brain: the men with guns searching the woods – and Gemeralda calling to them. He narrowed his eyes. "How do I know you'll help Flame-Red?"

"Of course I will!"

"You shouted to the men with guns."

"I got confused – I didn't know it was the SMI. Please let me out. I need your help. So does your mum." Her voice was sickly sweet.

Toby imagined arriving home to his mum and Witch Hazel that night and telling them everything. Mum wouldn't be pleased to see him, to know he'd deserted his friends. And she would hate to think of other people becoming as ill as her from the Life Source spell. She would want him to try and stop the SMI. She would want him to do what was right.

Flame-Red was searching the fields all by herself in the darkness. Bumble and Willow were captured and about to be shipped off to Denmark. And Gemeralda was up to something, that was for sure.

Toby turned his back firmly on the cabin and got into his sleeping bag. "I'm staying here."

CHAPTER TWENTY-SIX

When Toby awoke the next morning, Flame-Red lay fast asleep nearby. She was huddled deep inside her cloak, wild corkscrews of hair the only visible part. Marvin was curled by her side.

Toby filled his water bottle at a spring and approached the hole in the cabin wall. A bit more of the stone had crumbled away around it. He peered through: Gemeralda was awake but silent and made no mention of their night-time conversation.

He waited another hour before waking Flame-Red. Who knew when she'd returned. Eventually, he poked the mound of black cloak, and her face appeared wearing a scowl. She obviously wasn't a morning person. Although, to be honest, she wasn't really an 'any time of the day' type of person. He handed her the water, and bleary-eyed, she heaved herself onto her forearms and took a long drink.

"What time is it?" she mumbled.

"Nine o'clock."

"Nine o'clock!" Flame-Red sprang up. "We have to get on! We have so much to do."

171

"Did you find the…" Toby lowered his voice, "*ingredients*?"

She patted her pocket. "All here, potion made."

"Sleeping *and* memory potion?" he whispered. She'd been so unsure yesterday.

"Yes. I'm calling it *Dozify*. It took several attempts, and it got pretty hairy at one point." Flame-Red rubbed a hand over her forehead, and Toby did a double-take. One of her eyebrows was missing. He was about to say something, saw the warning glare on her face and thought better of it.

"You might find a rather dazed mouse wandering around later," she added.

"You tested it on a mouse?"

"The little thing will be fine – I dug it a hole till the effects wear off. But I had to know the potion worked. This is our one chance to rescue my mum, Bumble, and the wizards. We have to get it right."

During the time Toby had been considering running away, Flame-Red had been tramping alone through the countryside and making incredible potions. She was a force to be reckoned with.

"Ready for next steps?" he said.

"Ready for next steps," she replied.

Half an hour later, they alighted in the woods.

"There are about two hundred wizards," said Flame-Red. "Then there's four witches. Two people can fit on one broom, so we need one hundred and two broomsticks."

"That's a *lot* of broomsticks," said Toby.

"You cut the branches, and I'll shape them into brooms?"

Toby gazed upwards at the trees, some of which reached high into the sky. He gave a gulp. Climbing he was good at, heights not so much. Plus, his ankle was still healing. "How about *you* cut off the branches, and *I'll* shape them?"

Flame-Red shook her head. "Only witches can make brooms. Otherwise they won't fly."

"How wide do they need to be? My penknife's sharp but it won't cut through the thicker branches."

"Not that wide." Flame-Red put two of her fingers together and held them up. "This width, maybe?"

Toby flicked through the blades on his penknife and selected the serrated one. That should do it. Steeling himself, he got a foothold in a tree and hauled himself up. His ankle held firm.

There were quite a lot of thinner branches near the ground so it wasn't too bad finding the first fifty broomsticks. But that was half the number they needed. Jumping from the final tree, Toby wiped his palms on his jeans and scoured the woods. The rest of the trees with low-hanging branches were too close to the SMI. He'd have to be invisible, but every time he reached out his penknife, his bubble would burst. It was too risky. He would have to climb higher in these trees.

Flame-Red was sitting on the forest floor, using sharp stones to smooth the branches and fashion them into broomsticks. "Everything all right?"

Toby fixed a mask on his face. "Fine."

He stood at the base of a tree. As he summoned his courage, something Mum had once said echoed in his

173

mind: '*Don't see a problem as a mountain, see it as lots of little molehills. Take each molehill one at a time.*'

Toby placed his foot in a knot. Just this step. And then the next. This hand here. And that hand there. Now this step. And so he began to climb. As he clambered upwards, a ripple of excitement buzzed through him. Using your body to defy gravity was pretty awesome. He was practically Spiderman.

It was when he started to saw at the first branch that the nerves kicked in. He was hanging onto a tree trunk with one arm, five metres in the air, his feet balanced on precarious footholds. A particularly ferocious gust of wind chose that moment to tear through the treetops. Toby clung on like a baby monkey. He gritted his teeth. One saw of the knife, and then the next. One more, and the branch was dangling, attached by a single splinter of wood. Toby shoved his penknife into his pocket and grabbed the branch before it went crashing to Earth.

Now all he needed to do was get back to the ground. Easier said than done. Going down meant he had to look down. And he was holding a branch, leaving only one hand free to grasp the tree. Toby searched for a foothold, and his head swam. He was terrifyingly high. *Molehills, molehills,* said his mum in his mind. One step. Then another. This hand here. And that foot there. Slowly but surely, Toby edged down the tree.

He leapt the final metre, his legs wobbly but on firm ground. He had done it.

Flame-Red grinned at him. "That was high! Witchtastic work."

Toby gave a weak smile. Another fifty-one branches to go, but he could do this.

It was almost five p.m. by the time they'd finished. Toby's arms were scratched all over, and a layer of sweat coated his brow, even though it wasn't hot. But one hundred and two brooms lined the floor.

"They're not perfect," said Flame-Red. "And they'll be a bit unbalanced without twigs on the end, but I can't help that. They should get the wizards home at least."

"Do you think they'll return to Wildhaven?" Toby said.

Flame-Red picked her fingernail. "I don't know where they'll go. It won't be safe for them on the island now its location has been discovered."

"Maybe they'll move back to Little Witchery? You said you miss your dad and brother."

"Mum thinks living together is risky – a lot of the wizards supported Zazzle's uprising. And they didn't treat us as equals. They had all the important roles."

"But that means you split up families. Men and women manage fine on Earth together."

"And who has most of the important jobs?"

Toby opened his mouth to reply and then shut it again.

Flame-Red gave a knowing smile.

They spent the next hour flying armfuls of broomsticks to the field opposite the SMI. Every time they unloaded, their bubbles burst, and Toby darted an anxious glance towards the hill. But nobody appeared.

Eventually, one hundred and two brooms were piled against the wall.

"I hope no one finds them," said Flame-Red.

"I doubt they will," said Toby. "You can't see them

from the road. Anyway, they don't look like brooms without the twigs, just a pile of sticks."

He flopped on the grass.

Flame-Red poked him with her boot. "We don't have time to rest."

"I haven't stopped all day! You've been sitting."

"I hardly got any sleep last night! Unlike somebody else I could mention."

"Give me a few minutes," said Toby with a groan.

"You have two minutes," she said.

Toby lay back. The ground was muddy, but he was already dirty, a bit more wouldn't hurt. He must seriously pong – he hadn't washed in days. Unless you count the thunderstorm they got caught in.

As Flame-Red waited, she gazed at the SMI. "Not long now, Tally."

"Is Tally short for something?" asked Toby.

Flame-Red muttered, "Tallbridge Younger."

"He has the same name as your dad?"

"All witches and wizards take the name of their mum or dad for the first few years of their life. We get our own name when something in our personality or looks becomes especially noticeable."

No prize for guessing where Flame-Red's name had come from – she was always a spark about to ignite into fire. Or maybe she'd got her name from the colour of her hair? Probably both. So where did Bumble's come from? Because she bumbled around? Imagine being lumbered with that for the rest of your life just because of one particular characteristic.

Toby considered it. What name would he have been given if he'd been a wizard? Maybe something cool because he was good at running or sport. Wizard Sprint or Wizard Zoom. He paused. Or would they have named him after his white patch of hair? Wizard Tuft. *Ugh*, how awful would that be.

"Your two minutes are up," said Flame-Red.

As he hauled himself to his feet, the door in the SMI opened, and several people emerged. Flame-Red flicked her wand, and invisible bubbles sprang up around her and Toby. The group headed for the BMW parked inside the wall. Toby squinted across the road: the Director, Mr Dackman, Dacker, and one other. Four people. Four was all they'd seen in the SMI, right? So they'd all be at the Brocklehurst Hotel tonight, and no one would be guarding the SMI. *Perfect.*

"They're going already?" Flame-Red grabbed her broomstick. "I told you we needed to hurry! We better get Gemeralda. If we bring her here, we can make a quick departure once we've rescued the wizards."

Toby was about to say "*if* we rescue the wizards", but stopped. Flame-Red was getting more agitated by the minute, and it was best not to light the touchpaper just now.

They flew over the countryside. Buoyed by his success at climbing trees, Toby attempted again to remove his hands from Flame-Red's waist. He spread his arms for balance like he was walking a tightrope. *He was doing it. He was actually doing it*. A wide grin formed on his lips, and a clump of Flame-Red's hair stuck to his tongue. *Bleugh.* Amateur error. He hadn't done that for a while. He spat it out and lasted thirty whole seconds hands-free. *Not bad. Not bad at all.*

Landing at camp, Toby's small achievement was

177

instantly forgotten. Something was very wrong. Marvin was curled up asleep where they'd left him. But part of the cabin wall had crumbled. The cabin was empty.

Gemeralda had escaped.

CHAPTER TWENTY-SEVEN

"Where's she gone?" Flame-Red's head whipped from side to side. "If she doesn't come with us tonight, she may never find her way back to Little Witchery!"

She dashed round the other end of the cabin. *Deserted.*

The lake was still and silent, its dark surface reflecting the foreboding clouds above.

"I think it's my fault she's escaped," said Toby. "There was a small hole in the cabin wall last night. I assumed it had always been there. Gemeralda must have been chiselling away at it while we weren't here."

"Why didn't you say something?"

Toby edged backwards. "She can't have got far. She doesn't have her wand, so she won't be flying."

Flame-Red clasped her mouth. "Her wand! It was digging into my side in the night, so I took it out of my pocket … and I don't think I picked it up again this morning."

She dropped onto her knees, scouring the grass. There was no sign of Gemeralda's wand. "She must have taken it. What if she's going to ruin our plans?"

"I don't see why she'd do that. Surely she wants the wizards free?" said Toby.

Flame-Red was beginning to panic, clutching her wild hair and almost pulling out handfuls of curls.

Toby took her arms and looked into her eyes. "It'll be OK. We'll find Gemeralda later. But right now, we need to concentrate on getting to the hotel."

Flame-Red gave a weak smile and nodded.

Suddenly realising how close her face was, Toby released her arms as if he'd been stung.

"Let's go," he muttered and climbed onto the broom before Flame-Red had even mounted it herself.

She scooped up Marvin, and they took to the air.

They alighted in Brocklehurst market square to find a steady stream of people already filtering into the hotel. It was easy to tell which were the wizards. They might not have been wearing their black travelling cloaks, but they still stood out. A few sported long beards and hair which reached to their knees, and all of them wore eccentric clothing – some in tunics and most in stripy pyjama-like tops and trousers.

Marvin was awake now, and Flame-Red was struggling to hold him. "You can't get down here!" she hissed as he wriggled in her arms.

Across the square, a Jaguar purred to a stop. The chauffeur sprang from his seat, opened the door and out stepped the Prime Minister. Two bodyguards and a wizard followed him up the stairs to the hotel. The car drove away, leaving the village centre empty. It seemed all the invitees had arrived.

"I should be going," said Flame-Red. "You have the Dozify potion?"

Toby tapped his pocket and nodded. He had the urge to hug her, to briefly touch her shoulder, to reach out to her somehow. Flame-Red had a more perilous task than him – she was walking right into the dragon's lair.

He lifted an arm, changed his mind and dropped it again. He couldn't make contact with her anyway, it would burst their invisible screens. As he stood there awkwardly, Flame-Red raised her hand and placed it on the inside of her bubble. "High five!"

Toby smiled and held his palm against hers, on the inside of his own bubble. "High five!"

She gave him a wonky grin. She looked pretty ridiculous with her missing eyebrow, but for once, he had no desire to make fun of her.

"Best of stars," said Flame-Red.

"Best of stars?" repeated Toby.

"It means I hope it goes well."

"Oh, you mean good luck. Best of stars to you too."

Flame-Red wrapped Marvin firmly under her arm. "I'll see you soon then?"

Worries swirled around Toby. What if the plan didn't work? What if they were caught? Or worse, someone was hurt? He swallowed them down. "Yes, see you soon."

As the witch flew away, Toby felt a wrench. She might annoy him sometimes, but they'd spent almost every minute of the past five days together. They'd been a team. For once, he'd been able to share the burden of a problem. Now he was alone again. And this part of the mission rested entirely on his shoulders.

Toby took in a deep breath. He'd got this. He was used to solving things by himself. It was time to start the Great Wizard Rescue.

He tiptoed across the cobbles and past the fountain. The hotel was edged in on either side by buildings. On the left, however, a narrow passageway led to the back.

Perfect.

Toby was halfway along it when a door swung open. There came the clatter of pots and pans, and voices, and he froze. A heavenly aroma enveloped him. Beef, gravy … and what was that? Apple crumble? In a daze, he followed the rich scent, drinking it in.

When he was a few paces from the door, a woman in an apron stepped out. Toby's trance broke instantly, and he began to retreat. Fortunately, the woman veered to the right, threw a bulging bag into a bin at the end of the passage and returned to the kitchen. The door banged shut behind her.

Toby gave himself a shake. That had been close. He needed to forget his gurgling stomach. He'd deal with it later. Toby hurried past the door before anyone else could appear.

Round the back, light spilled from the hotel windows. They stretched the full length of the ground floor. Inside, the room was bustling. People in suits mingled, each of them flanked by a wizard. Nearly everyone was male. Flame-Red had been right – men *did* occupy most of the important jobs.

Snippets of conversation floated through the open windows:

"Oh yes, it's going very well …"

"I'm now the best shot at grouse hunting in the

country, thanks to a little help from a certain spell …"

"My mind is as sharp as a needle …"

"I can hear what my employees are saying from three rooms away …"

Toby scanned the crowd. There was Mr Dackman, looking as arrogant as always, and behind him hovered a wizard with a white beard and blue and white striped clothes. It was the man Toby had seen outside the Dackers' house when he'd lost his football! So that *had* been a wizard. Toby had known something was wrong.

Mr Dackman beckoned to Dacker, who was lingering by the door. The boy moved across the room so fast that Toby blinked and almost missed it. That could *not* be natural. Dacker *must* have gained superspeed from the Life Source spell. If all went to plan, there'd be no more Life Source spells for him, and no place on the Radton Rangers team either.

The Prime Minister stood in the centre of the room, surrounded by admirers vying for his attention. Mr Dackman elbowed his way through and extended a hand, then nudged his son to do the same. Dacker shot out his arm, knocking the Prime Minister's drink. Red-faced, Mr Dackman dragged Dacker away and gave him a hefty clout on the head.

"Sorry, Dad! Sorry." Dacker recoiled like he was expecting to be hit again.

Toby cringed. Darren Dackman may be his arch-enemy at school, but to see him treated like this by his own dad was a shock. Maybe having a father wasn't always great after all.

Toby altered his gaze, searching for Flame-Red's dad.

The room was packed. Surely, if all the wizards grabbed their wands from their captors at once, they'd be able to escape? They didn't even need the potion. Lords and Dukes and Prime Ministers wouldn't be able to fight back against magic. Then Toby saw why it wouldn't work. At either end of the room stood two men in camouflage gear, guns in their belts.

They couldn't continue with the rescue plan now! It was far too dangerous. Why hadn't they realised the army would be there too?

A glass door slid open, and Wizard Tallbridge stepped into the small garden. Right on cue. He walked along the lawn and disappeared into the shadows.

Toby followed. "I'm here," he hissed.

"I can't stay long," whispered the wizard. "I told Lord High-and-Monty I needed some fresh air. He wasn't best pleased; he thinks I should be on hand to deliver his every wish."

Toby snorted.

"You have the potion?" said Tallbridge.

"Yes, but have you seen the men with guns? It's too risky. They're not afraid to use them – you saw what they did to the wizard in your caves."

"We have no other choice. Unless we want to remain as servants or locked in cells for the rest of our lives." Tallbridge's voice was grim but steady. "The potion?"

Inside the vial, the thick, creamy Dozify liquid pulsated gently. Just watching it made Toby drowsy. After a long pause, he pushed it into the wizard's outstretched hand. As he did so, he burst his invisible cover. "Quick! Put it back."

"I'm afraid my good master has my wand,

remember?" Tallbridge said in a sarcastic tone. "You'll be fine. You have nothing else to do. Go straight to the meeting place. Flame-Red and the rest of the wyzine clan should be there shortly. I'll join you soon after … And thank you, Toby." He strode up the garden path and into the function room.

This was it. There was no going back now. Visible for all to see, Toby crept along the lawn. As he neared the windows, the hum of talking became audible once more, and he dropped to his knees out of sight.

"Jack Bean! Good to see you," boomed a voice from the hotel.

Toby's heart missed a beat. That name! He rarely came across anybody with his own surname, and he'd never heard anyone else called Jack Bean, not apart from his… *No.* He couldn't think about it; it was too painful. Toby peeped over the windowsill: a man was talking to the SMI Director. People called the Director JB – was that what it stood for? Jack Bean? The Director was full of smiles, throwing his arms round with animation as he talked; he clearly knew how to charm. Then he turned, facing away from the window.

Toby's head jerked back as if he'd been punched in the face. Above the nape of the Director's neck, amongst his brown hair, nestled a white tuft. Toby's hand strayed to his own identical white patch. Skylark had said something last year about the Director having one, but Toby had pushed it out of his mind – who wanted to have something in common with the killer of witches?

Toby's thoughts began to race, fuelled by his increasing pulse. How old was the Director? In his forties? And how old would the person-Toby-couldn't-

185

think-about be if he were still alive? The same.

The Director was called Jack Bean, he was the right age, and he had a white tuft of hair. It couldn't be? Could it? But Toby knew the answer. It was too much of a coincidence. The Director of the SMI was his dad. The man whom Toby thought had died when he was two, the man whom he'd never got the chance to know, the man whom he'd missed his whole life, was very much alive and standing right in front of him.

CHAPTER TWENTY-EIGHT

Toby shoved his fist into his mouth to stop all the emotion bubbling out in one enormous scream. All those years, his dad had been working at the SMI behind Toby's garden. Why had his dad never visited? Never even sent a card on his son's birthday? Didn't he care? All that time they could have spent together.

More thoughts pushed their way in, whizzing around Toby's mind. Mum had lied to him! '*Your dad died in a car crash,*' she'd said. '*Your dad died when you were two.*' No wonder she didn't like to talk about him. No wonder there were no photos, no keepsakes. '*We were a happy family,*' she'd said. Lies! All lies! Tears rolled down Toby's cheeks, and his shoulders shook uncontrollably. He slumped against the building, his head in his hands.

The sound of clapping forced him back to reality. How long had he been sitting there? Too long. He should be far away by now, away from any trouble to come. He peered over the windowsill once more. The Director was holding a glass in the air, expectant faces watching him. The last of the drinks were being filled from a giant bowl. Wizard Tallbridge hovered nearby, looking calm and

187

collected. He must have done it then. The potion must be in the drink.

Fear suddenly gripped Toby. His dad! He'd only just found him. What would the potion do to him? Flame-Red had said it would knock them out for a few hours and erase their short-term memory. But she'd only created it today – what if it went wrong? Toby couldn't let it happen. He'd wished for a dad for so long. He and Mum needed one. His dad could help pay for their food. Buy them a house without a leaking roof. What should Toby do? Intervene?

The Director cleared his throat. "Welcome," he announced, beaming at the crowd, "and thank you, everyone, for coming."

Something in Toby's pocket vibrated. His phone? No, he'd left it in his backpack by the broomsticks, and anyway, the battery had died. Gingerly, he reached into his pocket and pulled out a screwed-up tissue which was buzzing like an angry wasp. He unfolded it, and a small bottle fell into his palm. *The Alarmis potion!*

Inside, the silver coil spun wildly, the liquid frothing. The whole thing was vibrating stronger and stronger. It grew hot in Toby's hand, the contents pushing at the cork lid. It was going to blow. Toby threw it into the air. It sailed down the garden and exploded before it hit the ground. He threw his arm across his face as shards of glass rained upon him.

Flame-Red had nearly killed him! *Hang on* – Flame-Red – she had one of those bottles too. This meant she was calling for help.

In the hotel, the Director was still talking to the crowd. "We're gathered here tonight to celebrate the arrival of the wonderful wizards. We're so grateful for their assistance." He beamed and led a round of applause.

The wizards looked on stony-eyed, shoulders hunched.

Toby bristled. '*Grateful for their assistance*'? They were hardly willing participants. The lives of their families were at risk.

"Our magical friends are happy to put their powers to good use." The Director clasped Wizard Tallbridge's arm with steely fingers. "Aren't you?"

"Yes," mumbled Tallbridge.

A switch flicked in Toby. The Director's words were as fake as his smile. Father or not, Toby was better off without him. He and Mum could manage alone – they'd done so long enough.

He'd wasted enough time here. Flame-Red needed him. He might have only known her for a few days. Yes, she could be grumpy and stubborn, but she was also fun and full of energy. And she was thoughtful. She seemed to care. Unlike this man who was supposed to be his dad. This man didn't care about anyone but himself. Not the wizards he was enslaving, nor the people who were being drained of their energy.

The two soldiers stood at the end of the room, hands resting on their holsters. Toby shivered. "Good luck," he whispered in the direction of Wizard Tallbridge. Then he crawled under the windows till he reached the side passage.

He strode down it. Pots and pans clattered in the kitchen, but thankfully the door remained shut. Toby was desperate to run, but he was no longer invisible, and he mustn't draw attention to himself. Once through the small streets lined with cottages and on the country lane, he broke into a jog.

As he neared the SMI, two ear-splitting CRACKS ricocheted around the valley. Toby jumped violently. He scanned the sky: evening was drawing in, but there was no sign of black clouds. Not thunder then.

CRACK. There was no mistaking the direction it came from this time. Toby whipped around and peered back towards the Brocklehurst hotel. CRACK CRACK. *Gunshots*. Were Tallbridge and his fellow wizards in trouble?

Should he return? Try and help? No, he didn't have a gun or wand. Flame-Red needed him. He had to get to the SMI and make sure her part of the mission had been successful. If something had gone wrong at the hotel, the lives of the wizards in the dungeons were at stake. Toby sped down the lane as if the bullets were firing directly at him.

CHAPTER TWENTY-NINE

Toby vaulted over the stone wall opposite the SMI. The broomsticks they'd made that day were still neatly stacked in piles. And there was his backpack where he'd left it. But where was Flame-Red? She should be here with the wizards from the dungeons by now. Had something gone wrong? Is that why she'd contacted him via the Alarmis potion?

Toby scanned the field. Maybe they were invisible? He wouldn't be able to see them as he was no longer in a bubble.

"Flame? Flame-Red?" he hissed.

No reply. This was just like her. Any moment now, she would shout boo and scare the living daylights out of him. Toby stretched his arms in front and wandered around the field, grasping at the air, hoping to grab part of a body or clothing. He must have looked an absolute fool – like a zombie trying to catch its next meal.

He found no one.

Something brushed against Toby's legs, and he flinched. A beige snout and big eyes gazed up at him. *Marvin.*

"Where is she, boy? Where's Flame-Red?"

191

The fox scampered onto the stone wall. Fur bristling and tail pointed skywards, he stared in the direction of the SMI.

Something had clearly happened.

This wasn't part of the plan. He was only supposed to be responsible for the hotel mission. Flame-Red had said he wouldn't have to go anywhere near the SMI.

Toby took a deep breath. He'd promised his mum he wouldn't get into trouble, but Flame-Red needed his help. So did the wizards. So did every single person who was being used for the Life Source spell. And judging by the sound of the gunshots, he didn't have much time.

He pulled his baseball cap down firmly. He was going in.

Toby climbed over the wall and crossed the lane. The grassy mound loomed before him. Were there more traps around it? Like the one Willow and Bumble had fallen into? He heaved a loose slab from the wall and threw it in front. The ground stayed firm. He stepped forwards, seized the slab and threw it another metre. And so he went on, testing each bit of earth before treading on it.

Marvin darted ahead, and Toby cried, "No! Come here!"

The fox bounded back, scurried up Toby's legs and wound around his shoulders like a fur scarf. He was surprisingly heavy, but it was a comfort to have him there, even if his breath did smell of fish.

As they neared the door in the hill, Toby willed it to open, willed Flame-Red and the wizards to come pouring out. The rescue would have taken longer than expected – maybe Flame-Red's wand hadn't been able to open the dungeon doors. But the wizards would be free now, and that half of the plan, at least, would have been successful.

Not a soul emerged.

Toby threw the slab for the final time, and it landed by the door. He was about to move when the ground vibrated beneath his feet, and with a rumble, a gaping hole appeared. He sprang backwards. The gap must be two metres wide, and it was deep with smooth sides – if he fell in, he'd never get out.

He retreated several steps and inhaled deeply. It was just like the long jump at school, right? And he was good at that. Toby sprinted forwards, taking giant strides, and leapt into the air. As they soared over the hole, Marvin's claws gripped his shoulders. They landed, and Toby's head collided with the door frame.

Stars danced in his vision, and he sank to his knees, everything spinning. Marvin licked his ear. Toby lifted his head. He could not stop now. He rose unsteadily to his feet.

In the middle of the door was a large hole with melted edges. Flame-Red must have done it with the Meltisse potion. So she'd definitely entered the SMI. A broomstick leant against the wall. Was that hers too? Is that how she'd avoided the trap? She'd flown? But if her broomstick was here, she was still in the hill. Toby climbed through the hole.

Inside, bright lights glared down on a reception area with gleaming tiled floors. Everything was white and clinical, like the previous SMI building behind Toby's house. He shivered. A desk stood in the middle of the room, and on either side were several doors. *Director. Mr Dackman. Office supplies.* No sign of any dungeons.

A trail of muddy footprints led to a door at the back

193

– Flame-Red's? They only went one way and didn't return. She really *was* still here. What had gone wrong? It shouldn't have been too difficult to free the wizards since all the employees were at the hotel.

Toby followed the footprints and passed through the door. After the bright lights of the reception, the lamps here were dim, and he had to blink. He was in a giant cavern with stone walls and a high ceiling. It was like another world.

"Helllooo?" Toby said. The word reverberated round the roof, dislodging a shower of stones. He gritted his teeth. What was that the postman had said about the caves not being stable?

Toby crept down a flight of stone steps. Ahead hung a swing bridge made of flimsy wood and rope. It was the only way forwards.

Cautiously, he placed one foot on the bridge. It rocked from side to side, and he grabbed the rope handrail. Marvin whined in his ear. Beneath them stretched a chasm so dark and deep, Toby couldn't see the bottom.

Molehills, just molehills. One step, then another. He edged slowly on. Halfway across, his foot caught on some broken wood, and his whole leg slipped between the planks. His heart almost burst from his chest. The bridge swung wildly, and Marvin stood up on Toby's shoulders and tried to clamber onto his head.

"Marvin! MARVIN! Stop it. You're covering my eyes." With one hand clutching the rail and the other trying to disentangle Marvin's nails from his hair, Toby managed to right himself.

The fox clasped frantically to his head as Toby

194

inched along the rest of the bridge and collapsed with relief on the far side, sweat dripping from his brow. He was on a small stone platform with another door in front. Marvin jumped down and sniffed the bottom of the door. He caught a scent and scrabbled at the gap.

Toby opened the door an inch and peered round. A waft of stale air hit him full in the face. Through the gloom, he could see more stone steps, one set leading down and the other up. Marvin squirmed through the opening and threw himself at a door on the left.

"What? What is it?" Toby pushed open the door to reveal an office.

A desk covered in papers stood in the middle, and cupboards lined one wall. Huddled at the back of the room, her arms tied to a pipe, was a girl with wild orange curls.

Marvin scuttled over and dived into her lap.

"Flame!" said Toby.

"Toby! Behind you!" she cried.

He whipped round to find a wand trained on him. The woman holding it had long black tresses and green eyes. She was the spitting image of Gemeralda, though older and taller. *Witch Ebonia.* The witch who had tried to take the leadership from Willow. Gemeralda's mum.

What on earth was Ebonia doing here? She was supposed to be poorly in Little Witchery.

"Ah, Toby, the hero who saved Skylark." Ebonia's voice dripped with sarcasm. "So nice to meet you properly."

Toby's skin prickled. Wasn't she supposed to be on their side? So why was she pointing a wand at him, her eyes flashing menacingly?

"Don't move!" Ebonia said.

Not on their side, then.

She pointed her wand at a coil of metal.

Take this wire
Bind the boy tight
Tie his wrists
So he can't fight.

The cable rose off the desk like a snake summoned by its charmer. It slithered through the air and wrapped itself around Toby's wrists. He struggled and tried to break free, but it held him firm, a python engulfing its prey.

Ebonia motioned for Toby to walk backwards.

Could he try and knock the wand out of her hand? Make a run for it?

"Don't even think about it," she said as if reading his mind.

She pushed him to the ground next to Flame-Red, and the wire wrapped itself around the thick pipe, securing his wrists tightly behind his back.

"The Director will be here soon," said Ebonia. "He'll know what to do with you both." Then she flounced out of the room.

Fear pounded through Toby's veins. They were completely trapped. They'd never escape. What would happen to Mum without him? And what happened to boys found breaking into secret government organisations?

CHAPTER THIRTY

Toby turned to Flame-Red. "I don't understand. What's Ebonia doing here? I thought she hated Earthens!"

"I have no idea. But I told you Gemeralda was up to no good. It explains why she called to the soldiers in the woods. Why she had that flare. And the compass. She must have been trying to contact the SMI and get us captured."

"It doesn't make any sense," said Toby. "Why would witches be helping to capture other witches and wizards?"

"I'm as confused as you are." Flame-Red twisted a curl of Marvin's fur between her fingers. "She's even more wicked than I thought."

"Did you get to free any of the wizards?" asked Toby.

"Ebonia tied me up as soon as I got here. I thought all the employees were at the hotel. I forgot we'd heard a female voice."

"Me too."

"How did it go? Did the Dozify potion work?" said Flame-Red.

She looked at him expectantly, and Toby's spirits plummeted. "I'm not sure."

"Why? What happened?"

"Your dad got the potion into the drink, but… I heard gunshots on my way here."

"Gunshots?" The colour drained from Flame-Red's face.

"We don't know what it means." Toby attempted to shape his features into a reassuring look while his insides swam with doubts. "The plan might still have worked. The hotel could be full of sleeping people, and the wizards could be on their way right now."

"Or my dad and the rest of the wizards could be dead," said Flame-Red in a strangled voice.

Marvin raised his snout from her lap and licked her chin.

"And if the mission didn't work," she continued, "the lives of all the wizards in the dungeons are at risk too."

In his head, Toby added a silent, *and so are ours*.

He gave himself a shake. *Stop wallowing*. He'd got out of worse circumstances than this.

Toby peered behind them: their wrists were tied to a thick pipe on the wall. He wriggled his arms, and the wire bit into his flesh.

"I've been trying to do that for the past hour," said Flame-Red. "It doesn't work."

"Where are your potions? Can't you melt the wire?"

She shook her head gloomily. "I used the last of it on the main door."

"What about your wand?"

"Ebonia put it in a cupboard and locked the door."

Toby examined the desk. Sheets of paper were stacked in piles. There were pencils and pens, too – ideal to poke someone's eye out, but not to cut his wrists free. And as for the pot plant, that was as useful a weapon as a sausage.

There were no scissors or anything sharp. Toby had left his penknife in his bag by the brooms in the field. What idiot goes into combat without their penknife? Him apparently.

But wait, there was something else on the desk. A black cuboid. Was that a wand-thief? It must be the one the Director had used to take Willow and Bumble's wands. Had Ebonia brought it with her?

Toby wriggled down till he was lying on the cold tiles, his hands still attached to the piping. If he stretched himself as far as possible, he could just wrap the toes of his shoes around one of the desk legs. He pulled, and the desk scraped across the floor.

Toby froze at the noise, but Ebonia didn't appear.

"What are you doing?" whispered Flame-Red.

He dragged the desk further towards them. The wand-thief was now directly above them. How to reach it without hands? He gave the desk a sharp nudge, and its contents wobbled. He kicked it again, harder. The wand-thief toppled over the edge and landed on his crotch. Toby suppressed a cry and bit his tongue.

"A wand-thief!" said Flame-Red, seeming oblivious to his pain. "I've never seen one this close."

Toby nudged it onto the ground and flicked the switch with his knee. A low humming filled the room, and the cupboard in the corner started to rattle. It rocked back and forth, shaking as if it housed a raging tiger. Something slammed against its door. A large dent appeared in the wood, and the lock splintered.

With one last bang, the door burst open, and a sack flew towards them. As it sailed through the air, the top opened, and hundreds of wands whizzed out, attaching themselves to the wand-thief like darts. Doors swinging, the cupboard teetered on one edge, then fell over with a sickening crash.

Before Flame-Red could work out which was her wand, Ebonia whirled into the room, her long locks flying behind her. "I might have known you two would be trouble."

She snatched up the wand-thief.

There came a ping, and Ebonia pulled a phone from her pocket. "The Director is on his way. He'll be here shortly."

Toby exchanged a horrified glance with Flame-Red. The Director should be fast asleep on the floor of the Brocklehurst hotel. Their plan hadn't worked.

Toby eyed Ebonia. Could they persuade her to release them?

"Witch Ebonia," he began in the politest tone he could muster. "Why are you helping the SMI? I thought you wanted to fight Earthens and take power, not work with them?"

"That's none of your business," said Ebonia.

"It's *my* business!" Flame-Red said. "You've captured my mum."

"Your mum is a fool. Last year, I gave the wyline clan the chance to let me lead them to victory over Earth. But they chose to follow your mother and hide away in Little Witchery. So thanks to the SMI, I've found another way to gain control of this country. Did you know the Prime Minister is one of our clients? It's only a matter of time before he's under my command." A wicked smile played out on Ebonia's lips.

Toby shuddered.

"But how can you work with the SMI? It's enslaving us! Holding us captive." Flame-Red's cheeks blazed as red as her hair.

"Just like the wyline clan is holding *my* mother captive," said Ebonia.

"That's not the same!" cried Flame-Red.

"She's been imprisoned on a cloud for thirty years. I've spent most of my life as an orphan. Maybe now the rest of you will understand what it's like to have family members taken from you."

Toby's mind whirred. *Witch Zazzle.* The witch banished for an uprising. Gemeralda's grandmother. That meant she must be Ebonia's mother.

Ebonia spun on the spot. "Now, if you'll excuse me, I have things to be getting on with."

"Wait!" said Flame-Red. "Don't you want to know where Gemeralda is?"

Ebonia stiffened.

"She was spying on us, so we tied her up," continued Flame-Red.

"Tied her up! How dare you," spat Ebonia. "That explains why she didn't report back to me."

"Report back to you?" asked Toby.

"I knew the witches would find Wildhaven deserted and would send a search party to look for the wizards. Gemeralda had instructions to follow."

"She did," muttered Toby.

"My daughter was supposed to keep me updated on the search party's progress. I wondered why she didn't come when Willow was captured, but I see now, the Director was right. There were others still out there to keep an eye on."

"Yes, she had us to contend with," said Flame-Red. "And we got the better of her."

Ebonia advanced on Flame-Red, her nostrils flaring. "Is that so?"

Hackles raised, Marvin gave a warning growl.

Toby pressed himself into the wall. *Why was Flame-Red winding her up?*

He was about to give Flame-Red a big nudge to stop talking when he saw her hands. Behind her back, she was fiddling with a potion. But with her wrists bound, she was struggling to remove the lid.

"And where is my daughter now?" hissed Ebonia.

"Probably lost somewhere in the depths of the English countryside," said Toby. Keeping his eyes on the witch's wand, he moved closer to Flame-Red and took hold of the cork.

"What are you two up to?" Ebonia darted the last metre towards them.

Marvin launched himself from Flame-Red's lap, his teeth clamping onto Ebonia's sleeve. Ebonia shook her arm ferociously, but the fox hung on tight. At the same time, Toby felt the cork pop off the potion. Straining at the wire, Flame-Red hurled the blue concoction at Ebonia, and the entire contents spilled over her foot.

The effects were instantaneous. Ebonia began shrinking – first her foot, then her leg, then her whole body.

"Marvin, let go!" screamed Flame-Red.

But it was too late. Attached to Ebonia, Marvin

202

started shrinking too. Before long, Ebonia and Marvin were both the size of a milk bottle, then a pencil.

Anguish flooded Flame-Red's face. "They've had too much. I only meant to use a few drops, but I couldn't control it with my wrists tied."

"What have you done to me?" screeched Ebonia. It came out as a tiny squeak.

She and Marvin were now as small as a button, then a pinhead. And then they vanished altogether.

"Stay where you are!" shouted Flame-Red. "Or I'll never find you again. Marvin, STAY!"

She wrestled against her handcuffs, and a trickle of blood ran down her arm.

"Pass me your potion bag," said Toby.

"What?"

"Your potion bag. Quick, pass it to me."

Flame-Red did as he said.

Hands behind his back, Toby emptied the vials from the bag and tucked it between his skin and the wire. Then he shuffled to a join in the pipe and pulled. The wire dug into his flesh through the material but didn't cut him. He tugged and tugged with all his might. The pipe creaked and rattled, and with a loud pop, it broke in two.

A stream of water gushed out, soaking Toby's jumper. At least it wasn't electricity … he would have been fried in an instant.

Released from the pipe, the wire unravelled around his wrists and fell to the floor. Flame-Red manoeuvred herself to the gap, and in seconds she was free too.

She seized the bottle of Enlargio and splashed several drops where they'd last seen Ebonia and Marvin. Two dots appeared. By the time they were the size of a ping-pong ball, Ebonia was already shaking her fist. Flame-Red snatched her tiny wand off her before she could do any damage.

Reaching squirrel size, they stopped growing. Flame-Red trickled one more careful drop on Marvin, and in moments, he was back to normal. He gave a disgruntled yap and shook his fur from his head to the tip of his bushy tail.

"What about me?" squeaked Ebonia.

"You can stay like that for now," said Flame-Red.

Water was still pouring from the pipe and puddling around their ankles.

"We'd better put her somewhere higher." Toby scooped Ebonia up and placed her on the desk.

Flame-Red grabbed the wand-thief, which looked like a porcupine with all the wands attached to it. "Ready?"

"Let's go."

They splashed out of the office. Time to free the wizards. The Director could return at any minute. They didn't have a moment to lose.

CHAPTER THIRTY-ONE

Flame-Red stopped outside the door, hesitating between the two staircases. Water was flowing out of the office now and surging down the steps which led deeper underground.

"Best go that way first," said Toby. "Before it gets submerged."

On the very top stair, his foot slipped, and he slid all the way to the bottom like a wild flume ride.

"Careful!" Flame-Red pulled him to his feet. "We have enough problems without you breaking your leg."

Toby rubbed his back. *Ouch.* And now his trousers were soaking wet too. *Excellent.*

Flame-Red rushed on, and he sloshed behind, his sopping clothes weighing him down. They found themselves in a gloomy tunnel with stone walls and the occasional solitary lightbulb hanging from the ceiling.

Around a bend, Flame-Red skidded to a halt. On their right stood a door made of thick metal bars. Inside sat two elderly wizards. Unlike the dungeon where they'd spoken to the Head Wizard and Flame-Red's brother, this one had no window. The air was stuffy, and the one lamp gave a ghoulish glow.

Toby rattled the bars. *Locked.* He looked to Flame-Red.

She shook her head. "I told you! The Meltisse potion is all gone."

He motioned to her wand.

"I can't! You know I can't. I couldn't even unlock the front door, and that was a flat surface."

"You can! I've seen you do enough spells. We don't have another choice."

Flame-Red held her wand to the keyhole. Voice wavering, she chanted:

Turn this latch
Without key
Unlock the door
And set them free.

The lock creaked, and she pushed the door. It didn't budge. "I told you I can't do it!"

"You need to believe in yourself." Toby touched her shoulder. "You've got this."

Flame-Red inhaled deeply and let it out slowly. Gripping her wand firmly, she tried the spell again.

The door swung open, and her eyes widened in surprise. She held up the wand-thief. "I'm from the wyline clan. Are any of these wands yours?"

With bewildered looks, the two wizards shuffled forwards and placed their arms over the black box. Two wands trembled and shot into their owners' hands like magnets.

"You need to go upstairs." Toby pointed along the tunnel. "That way. If you find any wizards imprisoned,

206

let them out."

The men blinked at him. Their faces were lined with creases, and shadows hung under their eyes.

"We don't have much time. Hurry!" Flame-Red gave them a push.

They splashed away, their cloaks trailing in the water.

"Upstairs! Open any dungeons!" Toby called to their retreating backs.

Flame-Red had already moved onto the next cell.

They continued down the tunnel, opening doors and sending bemused wizards back the way they'd come. The water had reached their knees and was still rising; the pipe must come straight off the mains. Toby shivered. It was like taking a walk in a river, and it was so cold, it was seeping into his bones.

Marvin kept stopping to shake the water from his coat. A particularly strong surge gushed over him, and he scampered up Flame-Red's legs. He balanced on her shoulders, his wet fur sticking out at angles.

They waded on, the tunnel taking them deeper and deeper underground. Above, the lights had started to flicker.

"Th…There c…can't be many more dungeons, c…can there?" said Flame-Red through chattering teeth.

The water splashed against Toby's thighs. If they stayed here much longer, they'd be swimming. He glanced at the ceiling, and a much scarier thought hit him – if they stayed here much longer, they'd run out of air.

They rounded a corner to find a dead end and, on the right, a final iron door. Behind the bars, Bumble was standing on a stone bench, clutching the skirts of her

207

dress. Almost half of the multicoloured patches had now turned black. Water lapped around her ankles, and Barnaby fluttered above her head.

"Flame-Red! Toby!" she exclaimed. "Mercy me. I thought it was the end of my days."

Willow appeared from the shadows and approached the door. "Flame! Are you all right?"

Flame-Red raised her wand to the keyhole, and her arm trembled.

She must have performed the spell fifty times in the last twenty minutes. Why had her nerves returned? Then Toby saw it, the anxious glance towards her mum from the corner of her eye.

"You can do it," he whispered, before saying to Willow, "Can you step back a bit? Give her some room?"

Flame-Red clasped her wand, lifted her head and chanted the spell with only the teeniest of wavers. The door opened with a click.

Willow strode out and touched her daughter on the cheek. "Thank you, darling."

Bumble jumped off the bench, her dress flying up like a parachute to show a white petticoat and bloomers. Toby averted his eyes so quickly he strained his neck. She splashed over and grabbed Flame-Red and Toby under each arm. "I'm so grateful, I could squish you."

"You kind of already are," said Toby, his face squashed against her chest.

The lights gave one last flicker and plunged them into darkness. Willow and Bumble prised their wands from the wand-thief, and all three witches whispered a spell. Three rays shone from their wands.

"We have to get out of here!" cried Flame-Red.

They set off, wading up the tunnel. The water was hip height now, and they were fighting against the current. Willow marched in front. How did she make it look so easy? She was tall, and the water only came to her thighs, but she had to duck to avoid low-hanging rocks.

Bumble, it seemed, had decided to take a bouncing approach. With every spring, she sent small waves washing over Toby and Flame-Red. Marvin had clambered onto Flame-Red's head, and each time Barnaby swooped above, the fox tried to bat him with a paw.

They reached the stairs to find they'd been transformed into a waterfall. How were they ever going to climb them? Willow approached, but the churning water beat her back. She tried again and nearly lost her footing.

At the top hovered several wizards. One of them spotted the three rays from the witches' wands, grabbed another wizard's hand, and edged down a step. Gradually, wizard by wizard, stair by stair, they created a human chain. Toby, Flame-Red, Bumble, and Willow held hands too, and the straggle of wizards pulled them, slipping and sliding up the steps.

"Why are you still here?" shouted Toby over the gushing water. "You need to get out before the Director returns."

One of the wizards gesticulated towards the door to the cavern. Toby pushed past to find even more wizards crowded by the bridge. *Why weren't they moving?* "Go! Go!"

They were all staring ahead, wands poised. Toby fought through the throng. And there, in the middle of the bridge, stood the Director of the SMI, a gun in his hands.

CHAPTER THIRTY-TWO

Toby's heart almost escaped his mouth. They were out of time.

"Back to the cells!" yelled the Director, wielding his gun.

"They can't go back," said Toby. "The whole place is flooding."

"That's what they deserve. My colleagues' bodies are lying on the floor of the Brocklehurst hotel."

So the potion *had* worked. On most of them, at least. Was the Director the only one who'd broken free?

"They're not dead," said Toby. "They're sleeping."

A flicker of relief flashed across the Director's face. "Dead or not, your magic is dangerous. Back to the cells!"

"*I'm* not a wizard," said Toby.

The Director peered through the gloom. "Then who are you?"

Toby's voice caught in his throat. "I'm… I'm…" He took hold of his courage with both hands. "I'm your son."

A deathly silence fell in the cavern, so quiet Toby could hear the blood pounding in his ears.

"My… My what?" said the Director.

Toby lifted his baseball cap and turned his head to show his white tuft.

"T…Toby?" The Director's eyes widened with incredulity, and he lowered the gun. "What are you doing on their side? Come, join me."

Toby's heart splintered down the middle. How long had he wanted a father? Another person to be there for him and Mum. But his dad was too late. "You've had my whole life. All that time, I thought you were dead. And now you're asking me to join you?"

"I wanted to visit. Your mother wouldn't let me."

Toby's knees buckled, and he reached out blindly for something to grab onto, but his fingers closed around thin air. And then Flame-Red was by his side, clutching his arm, holding him up.

Mum wouldn't let his dad visit? Surely that wasn't true – was it?

"Toby, you belong with me." His dad opened his arms, and Toby wanted to run into them. To feel safe, to have someone else take control, to look after him.

But no, if his dad really cared, he wouldn't have left Toby and his mum to struggle alone. Not since she fell ill. She wouldn't have been able to stop his dad visiting if he'd wanted to.

Bumble took Toby's other arm, and he was the filling in a sandwich, protected by friends who cared for him more than his dad ever had.

Tears bubbled up, blurring Toby's vision. The door opened on the far side of the cavern. Was that a figure? Long hair. A glint of green. *Gemeralda?* Toby squinted through the shadows, blinking away the tears. The figure was gone.

212

"Come, Toby." The Director beckoned again. "Let us work together. We would be an amazing team. These creatures are holding you back. Your mum is holding you back."

Anger exploded in Toby. He was not like this man, this man who drained people of energy, making them as ill as Mum, and then wrote them off. He looked straight at the Director. "Never," he said.

The Director's eyes narrowed. "You're no son of mine!"

The words stabbed Toby like a knife into an already open wound. But Flame-Red and Bumble held tight to him, their warmth seeping into his skin despite his soaking clothes.

The Director raised his gun again. "Back! Back," he yelled.

With a screech, Barnaby dived for his head, digging his claws into the Director's scalp and darting upwards, hair clutched in his claws.

The Director took aim and fired.

"Nooooo!" shrieked Bumble.

The air was filled with high-pitched squeaking and the frantic flapping of black wings. Had Barnaby been hit? The gunshot ricocheted off the ceiling with a loud CRACK which reverberated around the cavern. The bat zoomed into Bumble's pocket, and Toby swallowed a huge gulp. The Director had missed.

And then the roof began to fall in. It started with a sprinkle of stones which narrowly missed the Director. Then more stones cascaded down, and everyone tried to dodge them. Behind Toby, the wizards on the platform sidestepped this way and that, the ones on the edges at risk of toppling off.

"Let us out!" Toby shouted.

"You can't trust magical beings!" said the Director. "They're going nowhere."

A rumble echoed around the roof, and a rock the size of a football plummeted towards them. As Toby watched, time seemed to slow.

The rock fell,

fell,

fell,

and struck the Director on the shoulder. His eyes widened in shock, and his arms flailed, the gun slipping from his grasp. He teetered on one leg, the bridge swinging violently.

For one long second, Toby faltered, and then he ran onto the bridge, his hand outstretched. He was too late. The Director plunged through the ropes and tumbled into the dark depths below.

Numbness spread through Toby. He'd found his dad only to lose him again. Toby's limbs stopped responding. His brain stopped working. It was his fault. If he'd moved straight away, he might have saved his dad. *His fault. His fault.*

Somebody grabbed him. "You need to move!"

Rocks were falling all around, but Toby stayed immobile. His body was too heavy, his mind too foggy. He was picked up and half carried, half dragged across the bridge. A falling stone grazed his forehead, and a trickle of blood ran down his cheek, but he barely noticed.

He stood as wizards streamed past.

Willow took him by the shoulder and gently steered him towards the door. "Time to leave."

Flame-Red slapped her palm over her mouth. "We forgot Ebonia!" She raced back along the swaying bridge.

"Flame!" shouted Willow.

The fear in her voice woke something in Toby. He felt himself struggling to the surface like he'd been underwater. His mind cleared. His limbs loosened. Flame-Red was disappearing back into the dungeons. He had to go after her.

He was about to step forwards when the whole cavern creaked, and half the roof tumbled from the sky. A tumult of rocks crashed down, breaking the bridge in two.

Flame-Red reappeared on the far side, her hair soaking and bedraggled – the dungeons must be fully submerged now. In her hand, she clutched Ebonia.

"Stay there!" called Willow.

What else could she do? The bridge was broken. There was no way across.

"Broomstick! We need a broomstick," cried Bumble hopping from foot to foot.

"There are some outside, but we don't have time!" Toby leant over the edge of the platform – the remains of the bridge hung from one fraying rope. He pulled it up and broke off a plank. "Can you make this fly?"

"Y…yes," said Willow. "But I'm not sure it'll take my weight."

"Can you make it fly with me on it?"

She set her jaw. "Yes."

Toby scrambled onto the wooden plank, and it rose into the air. He almost toppled straight off. Broomstick riding might have become easier, but this was a whole different flying game. What was he supposed to grip

215

onto? Panicking, he flapped his arms wildly.

Ahead, Flame's eyes were large and pleading.

He could do this. He *had* to do this. He'd practised hands-free on the broom yesterday, hadn't he? And he'd managed it.

Head up. Shoulders down. Balance.

Willow flew him on a winding path, dodging falling stones and clods of soil. Half kneeling, half sitting. Toby stayed stable and upright.

Reaching the other side, Flame-Red hauled herself on board. The plank dropped several feet, and Toby's stomach collided with his lungs. Flame-Red flung her arms around him; she was shivering uncontrollably. Or was that him? Or maybe it was both.

Bumble joined Willow, wand raised, and the plank rose then fell again. Moonlight shone through the hole in the roof, gleaming ghostly in the cavern, and somewhere far below lay the body of Toby's dad. Slowly, the plank hopped and bucked across the abyss.

A boom echoed round the cavern, so loud Toby's ears throbbed. The rest of the roof was caving in. Willow's face was rigid with concentration as she tried to steer them in safely. Bumble looked like she was about to pop a blood vessel in her brain.

With one last spurt, the plank kangarooed the final metre. They were going to make it. As Toby reached for Bumble's hand, a rock smashed into the end of the plank, breaking it in two. Toby and Flame-Red rocked violently, clinging to the rest of it. Then they were falling, the remains of the plank too small to take their weight.

"Noooo!" wailed Willow from above.

A bundle of beige fur launched itself from the

platform. Legs cycling in the air, Marvin plummeted down.

Eyes wide, he flapped his large ears. He continued dropping, falling faster than Toby, Flame-Red, and mini Ebonia. Furiously, he beat his ears, and then the most amazing thing happened: Marvin began to fly.

He sailed upwards, his tail circling like a windmill sail.

"Marvin! You can fly?" gasped Flame-Red.

The fox took Toby's jumper in his mouth and tugged hard. The momentum broke their fall.

With Marvin's ears beating strongly, and Willow and Bumble channelling all the magic they could muster, the remains of the plank gradually rose. It deposited Toby, Flame-Red, and Ebonia on the platform, and they slithered off in a heap.

Willow, the woman who never showed any emotion, seized her daughter and sobbed into her curls. "I thought I'd lost you."

Bumble bundled them all into her arms and dived through the door as the entire cavern collapsed with an earth-shattering roar.

CHAPTER THIRTY-THREE

Wet and dirty, Toby, Flame-Red, Willow, and Bumble stumbled through the reception area and into the night.

"B…be c…careful!" gasped Toby. "Th…there's a trap by the fr…front step."

But the hole was now covered with a plank of wood.

All the wizards were milling in the field across the road, already climbing onto broomsticks and soaring into the sky.

Marvin scampered over to Tally, who was huddled against Wizard Tallbridge. Flame-Red rushed to join them, and Willow strode after her.

A jolly-looking wizard in a tunic with stripes all colours of the rainbow sauntered over to Bumble.

"Wizard Merrycheeks! I'm so glad you're safe." Her cheeks blushed as red as Toby's favourite football shirt.

They regarded each other shyly and then hugged.

Toby stood watching all the families reunite, with a piece of his heart missing, lost forever in the cavern. His sodden clothes clung to his skin, and he shivered, wrapping his arms around himself.

Marvin brushed against his legs.

"Tally," said Flame-Red. "This is Toby. He's spellsparking. You'll like him."

Toby flushed, warmth spreading through his body. Coming from Flame-Red, that was high praise.

Tally gave him a shy smile.

"So the Director is your dad, huh?" said Flame-Red.

Toby scuffed the grass with the toe of his trainer. "I just found out."

Before she could ask more, there came the distant wail of sirens.

Tallbridge's eyes flicked down the road. "We need to leave this place."

"Did the Dozify potion not work?" said Flame-Red.

"It did, very well. But the armed guards didn't have drinks, and the Director was so busy talking that he realised what was happening before he drank it. He was the only one who escaped." Tallbridge paused. "We overcame the guards … but we lost two wizards."

A grim silence settled over the group.

"What is this potion you talk of?" said Willow.

"It appears," began Tallbridge, "our daughter is quite the potion expert."

Flame-Red glanced nervously at her mum.

Willow frowned. "Flame? Is this true? You shouldn't be creating concoctions!"

"She's good at them!" said Toby. "She saved us from Ebonia by turning her tiny."

Wizard Tallbridge placed his hand on Willow's arm. "We should give her a chance."

Willow rubbed her forehead. "How did I not even know you were a potion witch? I get so tied up with running Little Witchery that I've been neglecting you.

And then I nearly lost you. Why don't we discuss this when we're home?"

Flame-Red gave a small nod. "Thanks, Mum." She held out the red ring. "I kept it safe for you."

"I see you didn't listen to it." Willow gave a wry smile.

"You told us to fetch help from Little Witchery – how could we without a warbler?"

"I attached my warbler round Barnaby's neck."

"Oh. OH!" said Flame-Red. "It must have fallen off."

"I shouldn't have doubted you. You did well."

As they looked at each other awkwardly, the last of Toby's jealousy dissolved. Flame-Red might have both parents, but neither of them knew anything about her. Toby might only have his mum, and she might be ill, but she was always there for him. She was his number one support, and she knew him inside out.

The earth vibrated beneath their feet, and with a low rumble, the rest of the SMI vanished into the ground. A giant plume of dirt and dust swirled from the crater.

"Time to go," said Tallbridge.

"Where's Ebonia?" said Flame-Red, looking this way and that. "I put her on the grass."

Willow narrowed her eyes. "I doubt she'll dare show her face in Little Witchery again."

"Gemeralda is probably somewhere around here, too," Flame-Red added.

"I think I may have seen her in the SMI – on the edge of the cavern. I can't be sure, but she had a broom and, when the Director…" Willow faltered. "Probably best not to speculate."

Toby studied her face. What was she suggesting? In the woods, two glints of emerald caught his attention. He screwed up his eyes. Was that two figures or just the moonlight reflecting off the leaves?

The sirens grew louder. The last of the wizards and witches grabbed broomsticks and climbed on.

Toby hesitated. Did they want him with them? Now they knew the Director was his dad?

"What are you waiting for?" said Flame-Red, pulling him onto her broom.

He put his arms around her waist, and they rose into the air.

As they flew over Brocklehurst, people were staggering out of the hotel, rubbing their eyes.

"Wh…what happened?" said one.

"Who are you?" said another. "Wait, who am I?"

Lord Montgomery stumbled across the market square, his face dazed, and his black suit ripped. "What the blazes is going on? I won't be treated like this! Do you hear me?" he shouted to no one in particular. "Where even am I?" He swung round, fell over his walking stick and toppled head-first into the fountain.

In front of Toby, Flame-Red let out an explosive giggle.

They soared higher into the sky, leaving the remains of the SMI and its dastardly accomplices far, far behind.

221

CHAPTER THIRTY-FOUR

Later that night, Toby, Flame-Red, and Bumble crept into Toby's house.

"Keep quiet," he whispered. "My mum will be asleep."

Bumble promptly bumped against the kitchen table, and a chair fell over. The three of them froze, but the house remained silent. They tiptoed into the lounge and collapsed onto the sofa and armchairs. Witch Hazel was using Toby's room as the guest room that week. He smiled at the thought of her surrounded by football posters and curled up under his blue and white Radton Rangers duvet.

Toby tried to get comfortable. Bumble had magically lengthened his armchair, but several springs now poked out of the cushion. They definitely hadn't been there before she'd waved her wand at it. At least it was better than sleeping on the ground.

The three of them were still draped around the lounge when Hazel wandered in the next morning, yawning and smoothing her lilac dress. She stopped abruptly. "We weren't expecting you back for another two days!"

Toby rubbed his eyes. "It's a long story, a very long story."

While Flame-Red and Bumble told Hazel everything, Toby climbed the stairs. Mum didn't have much energy to talk in the mornings, but he couldn't wait. He had questions that needed answering. He took a deep breath and pushed open her door.

She was sitting propped up against her pillows. "Toby! What are you doing home?"

"The SMI captured the wizards."

Her hand flew to her mouth. "I wondered why you weren't replying to my texts! I knew you were hiding something."

"It's OK. We got them out."

"My love, are you all right?" His mum opened her arms.

Toby stayed where he was.

"What's wrong?" she said.

"I know who he is."

His mum frowned. "Who 'who' is?"

"The Director of the SMI. I know who he is."

The blood drained from his mum's face. She was already pale, but now she was as white as a ghost.

"Why did you never tell me?" cried Toby. "All those years I thought my dad was dead!"

"Oh, Toby, I'm so sorry." Her voice wobbled. "He left us … for another woman. He didn't visit, didn't even send a card on your birthday. I decided it was best for you to think he was no longer alive." His mum's face crumpled. "I did what I thought was best – to protect you."

"He said he wanted to visit and you wouldn't let

223

him."

"I wish that were true. But he never tried to, not once. I'm so sorry, love."

"You saw him every day at work at the SMI!"

His mum flinched. "I kept as far away from him as possible. I used to love him. It was hard not to. He's a charismatic man; he can charm anybody. I didn't want to have to see him once he left, but he gave me the best wage I could get. I think it was to compensate for his guilt."

Toby studied the carpet. He knew Mum was telling the truth. But that meant his dad had been in the same street every single day and hadn't once attempted to see his own son. His dad really had never cared for him.

"Come here, love," said his mum.

"There's another thing," said Toby. "We were in a cavern, and h…he fell. Really far. I… I don't think he survived."

"You mean h…he's dead?" Tears trickled down her cheeks.

"It's my fault! If I hadn't hesitated, I might have been able to save him." Toby slumped onto the bed next to her.

She stroked his hair. "It is NOT your fault. None of this is your fault."

Toby began to cry too, big fat snotty tears. And they lay there together sobbing.

Half an hour later, Witch Hazel bustled into the bedroom, carrying a tray laden with toast. "I think you both need a jolly good breakfast."

Toby studied the bread. It looked good – lightly

browned and buttered to the edges. Had Hazel finally got the hang of Earthen cooking?

He took a bite and almost spat it out. The underside was burnt to a blackened crisp. He caught his mum's eye, and they tried not to laugh.

Witch Hazel didn't seem to have noticed. She was busy adjusting his mum's pillows and handing her a glass of water.

"Hazel?" said Toby.

"Yes, dear?"

"Flame told me how witches and wizards got their names. How did you get yours?"

"Ah." Witch Hazel's eyes twinkled with pride. "It's because I'm a Protector, you see. I care for sick witches. They saw that quality in me right back when I was little."

"So Hazel means Protector?" said Toby.

Witch Hazel smiled. "Not exactly. You know that my grandmother spent some years living on Earth before the wyline clan moved to Little Witchery in the sky?"

Toby nodded.

"Well, there's an Earthen plant called witch hazel. It's medicinal. It works wonders on many things, like soothing bruises and swellings. So, when I was growing up, my grandmother knew just what I should be called."

Witch Hazel stopped, her cheeks blushing.

"I think it suits you," said Toby and gave her a spontaneous hug which seemed to catch her by as much surprise as it did him.

"I'm glad you're home safe," she said, squeezing him.

"Me too." And it was true. This house may be small and falling apart, but it was much better than living in a

225

field, and much, much better than a dungeon. It was better than living in a cave on an island and even better than living in an empty mansion, however luxurious it was.

Because wasn't it actually the people in a house which made it a home? These days, it wasn't just him and Mum. Sometimes family wasn't who you were related to; sometimes it was who you chose. Not that Toby was sure he'd ever chosen the witches, they seemed to have chosen him. But his family was growing. The witches may cause him trouble at times, a LOT of trouble, but they also filled his life with colour and warmth. Maybe this house wasn't so bad after all.

CHAPTER THIRTY-FIVE

A week later, Toby opened the front door to find Flame-Red there.

"Surprise!" she said.

He frowned. "What are you doing here?"

"Mum's given me permission to spend the day with you on Earthen soil. How about we go on an outing?"

"Are you sure Willow is allowing it? I thought it was too dangerous for witches down here?"

"As long as we go somewhere quiet, she's said I can." Flame-Red shot him a smile that was way too innocent.

"What are you hiding from m–?"

"Nothing!" she said before he'd even finished his question.

"I'm not flying," said Toby. "I've had enough of broomsticks to last a hundred years."

He wheeled his bicycle out of their ramshackle shed, and Flame-Red stared at it. "There's no way I'm travelling on that spindly contraption."

So they set off, Toby cycling and Flame-Red flying somewhere above.

As Toby pedalled out of town, he passed Dacker on his skateboard. Dacker wobbled, and the skateboard flew out from under his feet. He chased after it and only just caught it before it rolled into the road. Toby suppressed a grin. So much for Dacker's superspeed. Radton Rangers had announced the squad yesterday, and Dacker hadn't been on the list. *No surprise there.* Toby's striker position was safe.

Summer had finally turned warm and sunny, and they spent the day exploring woods and paddling in streams. It was good to have company – Roger and Jazz weren't due back from Mauritius for another week.

"How's Little Witchery?" asked Toby as they leant against trees, basking in the heat.

"Ebonia and Gemeralda haven't returned. I guess they've remained on Earth."

Toby stiffened and glanced behind.

Flame-Red threw a handful of grass at him with a laugh. "They're not here! Brocklehurst is hundreds of skytracks away. Besides, they don't know where you live."

"What's happening with the wizards?"

"They might stay in Little Witchery. If the potion worked at the hotel, everyone involved should have forgotten all about wizards and magic. But it still doesn't feel safe for them to return to Wildhaven."

"You think you can cope with men among you?" said Toby. "I thought we took all the best jobs."

Flame-Red gave him a death stare. "With my mum in charge, we'll manage fine. Anyway, the Wyline Council has put new magical safeguards in place to prevent further uprisings."

228

"Must be nice to have your dad and brother with you."

"It is. And Mum is letting me take lessons with one of the wizards who's a master of potions."

"Brilliant!"

Flame-Red sighed. "She's making me take extra spell lessons, too though, so I don't fall behind."

They fell quiet for a while before Toby said, "Do you think Lord Montgomery's servant will be OK? The one who had the Life Source spell performed on her?"

"She should be fine. She didn't undergo it enough times to be permanently weakened."

Toby let out a long breath of relief. He couldn't make Mum better. But he'd saved this woman from suffering a similar fate, from losing her life, from being bedbound. Plus, hundreds of others too. Not being able to fix Mum made him feel pretty hopeless at times. But this, this he had done.

He stretched his legs in the sun and waggled his toes. Football would be starting again soon, and he was itching to get back.

Willow had lent Flame-Red a warbler for the day, and as the afternoon wore on, Flame-Red kept checking the screen.

"Are you waiting for something?" asked Toby when she examined it for the umpteenth time.

"No." She pushed it into her pocket.

"Shall we head back?"

"Not yet!" she said hurriedly. The sun had brought out her freckles, and she looked even more cheeky than normal. It was hard to tell if she was keeping something from him or not.

Out of nowhere, a boom of thunder shook the sky.

Flame-Red flinched. "No clouds, no rain."

"You don't think…?" said Toby.

"Witch Zazzle?" Flame-Red's forehead furrowed. "I don't know. I've been wondering if Ebonia and Gemeralda would try and break her free."

"What's keeping her imprisoned?"

"Cloud ghouls."

Cloud ghouls? Toby studied Flame-Red's face for any hint of mischief, but her expression was deadly serious.

Her warbler lit up. She put the tip of her wand to it and read the screen.

"What does it say?" said Toby.

"Nothing! Shall we go now?"

She was *definitely* hiding something.

Arriving home, Toby hadn't even dismounted his bike before the front door flew open.

"Come in! Come in," Bumble stood there, bouncing with excitement.

The front door led directly into the tiny lounge, which was brimming with Witch Hazel, Witch Willow, and Wizard Tallbridge.

Flame-Red crowded in behind him. "Surprise!"

From the ceiling hung a banner which read '*Thank you, Toby*'. It shimmered and flapped, transforming from blue to green to purple, while sparks danced around it.

Willow cleared her throat. "Toby, we wanted to thank you for all your help."

"Again," piped up Hazel from the back.

230

"If it were not for you," said Willow, "we would be languishing our days away in dungeons. Or as servants to royal families."

Toby shuffled his feet awkwardly. "It's fine," he muttered. "You didn't have to do this."

"You haven't seen anything yet!" Bumble grabbed his arm and propelled him into the kitchen.

Toby's mouth fell open. The room was two, no, three times the size it had been.

"We thought it best not to change the front room," said Willow. "We didn't want to rouse the suspicions of any Earthen visitors. But the rest of the house … well, you'll see."

Every surface in the kitchen gleamed. Gone were the peeling cupboards, scraped paint, and chipped tiles. Over the sink hovered a sponge. Hazel placed a dirty plate under it, and the sponge dived into action, scrubbing and cleaning. She threw a handful of crumbs onto the side, and a cloth flew to collect them, depositing them in the bin.

"You don't have to wash the dishes ever again." Bumble clapped in delight, and her dress billowed. It was back to a rainbow of colours without a black patch in sight.

"And there's more!" She pointed to a new appliance. "That button gives you instant hot water, that one cold water, and this one…" She pressed the button, "…frozen balls!"

A cascade of ice cubes fell onto the floor. "Flapping fluttermice, I forgot to put a glass there."

Toby stared around the kitchen. They'd done all this for him? And then his eyes fell on the table, piled high with food. All the worry over the last year rose inside him and got stuck in his throat. "How… how?"

The witches had said they wouldn't magic money. Had they changed their mind?

Flame-Red's cheeks flushed. "I've created a new potion which doubles the size of food. And it's safe to eat."

Willow placed her hand on her daughter's shoulder, her usually unreadable face filled with pride.

Bumble threw open a cupboard like a conjurer revealing a magic trick. Toby half expected her to say "Abracadabra!" Inside were rows of tiny bottles.

"Th…thank you." He sank into a chair. Things were going to be *so* much easier now.

"That's not everything!" said Bumble with a giant beam.

Tallbridge rapped three times on the fridge, and it slid away with a scraping noise. Behind stood a door. Bumble gestured for Toby to open it.

He stepped through into a large room. Hang on, that didn't make sense. How was there space for it? The neighbour's house was supposed to be here. There were no other doors leading off. There weren't any windows either.

The room was dimly lit, and Toby walked in further. Shapes emerged from the shadows. Shapes that turned out to be the most amazing things. A football table, a table tennis table, a basketball hoop, a sweet dispenser, and at the far end, a giant television screen with two comfy chairs. It was the stuff of dreams. "Is this…" he began.

"It's all yours, Toby." Hazel said softly.

"I'm sorry we didn't think to improve your living

arrangements sooner," said Willow. "I've been so caught up with Little Witchery affairs that I've neglected you as well as my daughter."

Toby threw himself into one of the chairs with a whoop of delight. It swung round, and he nearly bounced straight out of it. He was going to have so much fun in here. Roger and Jazz would absolutely love it … Toby stopped. He couldn't tell them about it. He had to keep the witches and magic a secret. His spirits plummeted. Where was the fun in having all this to himself?

Willow stepped forwards. "Flame-Red has permission to visit once a fortnight."

"I do?" Flame-Red's eyes went as round as a warbler. "Really?"

"Providing you keep up your spell lessons."

Toby stood by the football table. "Want a game?"

"You're on," said Flame-Red. "What do I have to do?"

"Get the ball in the goal. You'll lose."

"We'll see about that, Mr Blond Streak."

"Oh, yeah, Mrs Missing Eyebrow?"

They smirked at each other and started spinning their players furiously.

Later, when the witches had left, Toby climbed the stairs. Flame had won – three games to two. How had he let that happen?

He peeked round Mum's door. She was lying flat on her back, burrowed in the duvet.

"Must have been a lot for you today?" he said.

She smiled weakly. "Much quicker and quieter than

233

Earthen builders. How is it?"

"It's the most wonderful witchtastic thing I've ever seen."

A grin spread across his mum's lips.

Toby looked around her room. The walls had been repainted, but nothing much else had changed. "Sorry your room's not much better."

"The roof's fixed!" She pointed at the ceiling. "And that's not all. Open the curtains."

He drew them apart and gaped. The window had been replaced with a glass door, and beyond there was a balcony. "You can get outside if you're well enough!"

This was a hundred times better than his games room. Mum hadn't been in fresh air for over three years. She must have forgotten what it felt like to have warming sunrays on her skin. Toby peered beyond the balcony and was met with a dismal view of their concrete yard.

"Step back a moment." His mum pressed a button by her pillow.

The scene outside blurred and dissolved, and a new landscape emerged: a lake and, beyond, a range of mountain peaks. A pink sunset sparkled on the horizon.

There had been a LOT of surprises that evening, but this one was too much to get Toby's head round. He sank onto the bed. What was even real anymore?

His mum pressed the button again, and the scene became a sandy beach with turquoise waves lapping on the shore. Palm trees swayed in the breeze, and the smell of salt air floated in.

"Not bad, hey?" said his mum, a twinkle in her eye.

Toby opened his mouth and shut it again, words failing him.

"We can go on holiday together after all – without even leaving my bed. Where do you fancy tomorrow?

Rainforest? Egyptian pyramids?" His mum rested her head on her pillow and inhaled deeply.

Toby opened his arms to the sky and laughed and laughed and laughed. Yes, he may not have chosen the witches for his family. And they may have almost got him locked up. AGAIN. But they were a pretty awesome adoptive family. He was lucky to have them. As long as they didn't get him into any more trouble. But that wouldn't happen. The SMI was well and truly destroyed this time – wasn't it?

KEEP AN EYE OUT FOR THE

THIRD AND FINAL BOOK

IN THE SERIES

COMING 2025

ABOUT THE AUTHOR

Sally Doherty lives in leafy Surrey with her husband and three-legged (but speedy) rescue dog. After studying French and German at university, she worked for a year in London before unexpectedly falling ill with M.E. Being stuck at home and often in bed for over seventeen years, however, has lit a cauldron of stories bubbling inside her imagination.

FOLLOW SALLY ONLINE

Twitter
@Sally_writes

Facebook page
www.facebook.com/sallydohertywrites

Join the Facebook group for behind-the-scenes insight
Search for: The Toby Bean Trilogy

Instagram
@sallydohertywrites

Website
www.sallydohertyauthor.com

Sign up to the newsletter on the website to be the first to
hear about giveaways and book three!

ACKNOWLEDGEMENTS

Where to even begin? I have all the people from my previous acknowledgements to thank, as well as a whole bunch of new people!

Above all, my dad. For all his love, support, and laughter throughout my life. Dad, we never expected to lose you last year, and I still can't believe you're gone. But I'm so grateful for all the time I had with you, and I will cherish the memories forever.

My mum. Not only for all your editing wisdom, but also for turning out to be a pretty super duper sales person. Thank you so much for all the time you have spent helping to get my first book into the world and pushing me to make my second book better. And as for the way you are currently handling life, you could not be more amazing and I'm behind you all the way.

My husband. Thank you for being my rock. For doing everything around the house so I can use my tiny energy for writing. And for your kindness and humour. (PS. I am still waiting for you to read Toby one.)

My sister and nephew. What a year. I'm so grateful to have you both in my life.

My childhood and university friends and family-in-law. Becky, Hayley, Emily, Katie, Fiona, Clare, Lucy, Maggie and Shaun. For supporting me and my book so much. From sharing my posts on social media to buying several copies for friends. And above all, for being there for me through the difficult past year.

My writing friends. Anna B, Marisa, Emma B, Stuart and all of Rebel Alliance. As well as so many lovely Twitter pals. Interacting with you each day gets me through the fatigue!

My illustrator. Sarah Jane Docker. For creating yet another gorgeous cover as well as the internal illustrations. Each time, you turn my ideas into something better than I could have imagined.

My beta readers. Marisa, Emma D, Emma A, Sam and Jess. Thank you for your time and insightful advice.

The lovely people who read an early copy and provided quotes. Lisette Auton, Jenny Moore, Kate Heap, Emma D, Mr Tarrant.

All the teachers, TAs, librarians, bookshops, and bloggers who have supported me during my first year and a half of publication. Too many to name but here are a few: Ashley Booth at A New Chapter Books, Hope Cove Gallery, The Cider Press, Wonderland Bookshop, The Rocketship Bookshop, Through the Wardrobe Books, Fourbears Books, Arcturus Books, Books and Banter, Melissa at Readers That Care, Kate Heap, Amy at Golden Books Girl, Tony Britton at the ME Association, Jo Clarke. I'm so grateful for all your support.

And lastly, you, my reader, if you have got this far. To all of you who have read and enjoyed both my books. And for spreading the word and leaving reviews. It really makes such a difference. Thank you.